*Pride Publishing books by Ash Penn*

**Single title**
Loathing Leo
Chasing the Dragon
Moving On
Rent Mate

**Dark Love**
End of the Line

I0542318

# ME AND YOU TWO

ASH PENN

Me and You Two
ISBN # 978-1-78686-384-3
©Copyright Ash Penn 2019
Cover Art by Erin Dameron-Hill ©Copyright January 2019
Interior text design by Claire Siemaszkiewicz
Pride Publishing

Published in 2019 by Pride Publishing, United Kingdom.

Pride Publishing is an imprint of Totally Entwined Group Limited.

# ME AND YOU TWO

# Chapter One

"Hi, Dean." A girlish giggle accompanied the greeting, sweet enough to strip the enamel from my teeth.

I cracked open an eye. The blonde I'd spend most of the week hooked up with was standing before my sun lounger, dressed for the pool in a tiny bikini top and even tinier denim shorts. Her ash-blonde hair shimmered under a mid-morning sun.

"Good morning, ladies." Brian produced his best gap-toothed grin as he sidled over to the girls. He took care to lock his hands – and his wedding ring – behind his back. "Looks as though it's going to be another beaut. Not as lovely as the both of you, naturally."

Stacey gave him a wide berth and approached my sun lounger. Her slight but dense shadow chilled my bare chest, which had only partially cultivated a tan. "You do remember I'm leaving today?"

I'd done better than that. I'd assumed she'd already gone. As far as I was concerned, we'd said our goodbyes the night before, with a few hundred holiday-makers and a good length of bar-top between us.

"Yeah." I stifled a yawn. "Like I said last night, might see you next year."

Stacey pouted. "You still have my number, don't you? Only you said we could meet up after you finished work last night, and you didn't call."

She'd given me her number at the beginning of the week, but I'd deleted it last night after we'd said our goodbyes. Not that I didn't appreciate Stacey, or any of the others I'd hooked up with over the course of the summer. It was just that I was incapable of feeling anything for her—or them—despite almost always being able to convince them otherwise.

I grabbed my cigarettes from the grass. "I had a family emergency."

"Oh? Anything serious?" She sank to her knees and pressed a neat hand to my thigh. Pink nail varnish and a cheap ring glinting fake stones. I recalled that same hand working the base of my cock at the back of the clubhouse a few nights before. The memory of her roving tongue quivered through me, as did the thought of spending any more time in her company, but for entirely different reasons. "I might've been able to help."

"Nothing you could have done." Mainly because I hadn't seen my so-called family in two years, and if I didn't see them for another two, I'd call that a result. "It's all sorted now, anyway."

"I'm glad to hear it." She shifted her hand from my thigh to adjust her bikini top over her B cups. "Do you want to come to the pool with us?"

"Can't. Sorry." I lit my cigarette and inhaled a hefty drag. "I'm off out in a bit."

"Anywhere nice? I'm on a late checkout, so I can ditch the pool and come with."

I looked to Brian for rescue. Some hope. The park's maintenance manager was too busy schmoozing the girl I hadn't had, who was backing away from the ghoulish gawk pinned to her chest. Any rescuing was down to me. "Hey, Bri?"

Brian hitched up his low-slung overalls over his fat arse with one hand and made a batting gesture at me with the other.

I reached for my mobile. "Brian, mate. Your wife wants a word."

"What?" Brian spun around, almost tipping head first into the side of my caravan.

I placed my hand over Stacey's. "You'd better get your friend to safety. I'll see if I can pop by your van later."

She brightened with a smile far prettier than her pout. "Promise?"

"Remind me of the number again?"

"One hundred and eighteen, by the trees over there." She pointed down the path, though I knew the exact location of all the vans. I should do, I'd spent enough years in exile here.

"How do you have my wife's number?" Brian loomed above me, but at least he was done doing the same over Stacey's less-than-enthusiastic friend.

"I don't." I showed him the blank screen of my phone. "Now shut up and have a fag, before you get reported for sexual misconduct."

Stacey giggled, then planted a warm, unexpected kiss on my cheek before taking off after her pal.

Brian snatched a smoke from the packet and waited until the girls were out of earshot before passing comment. "How come it's all right for you to soak your wick willy-nilly, but when I want in on some action, the guests are off-limits?"

"That'll be because I haven't been married for the best part of twenty-odd years." I blew out a smoke ring. "And cut the attitude, or have you forgotten you're technically talking to your boss?"

Brian swiped my lighter from my fingers. "Boy, I got *technical* skid marks older than you."

"Yeah, and if you want your Linda to carry on scrubbing them from your budgie smugglers, I suggest you save your wick for her rather than…" I nodded in the general direction the girls had disappeared into.

"Where my wife is concerned, ignorance is bliss." Brian let out a sly chuckle as he handed back the lighter. "What's your career choice today, anyway? Marriage guidance counselor?"

I didn't answer. Something had distracted me. The dull scrape of plastic on tarmac. A lad came into view, strolling along the tarmac path tugging a cart behind him, loaded with a vacuum cleaner and bucket of cleaning products. He trundled along, pausing at the caravan across from mine, checking the number in the window, before moving along to the next.

"Hey."

He stopped. Homed in on me from behind a pair of black-framed geek glasses. Damned if he didn't have the sweetest face I'd seen in quite a while. Rounded cheeks and a pixie nose dotted with sandy freckles. I could only imagine his lower cheeks were equally plump.

I flicked my cigarette to the grass then sat up. "You looking for something?"

"Yes." The lad stared at me, rabbit-in-the-headlights style. "Number sixty-eight."

At the sound of his soft tone, my dick jerked in my pants.

Almost as if he could hear the testosterone raging through my balls, his gaze tracked to my fly. His lips tilted into a smirk—or a nervous smile. I couldn't tell which. So that made him one of two things. A wanton slut in the sack or as genuine a virgin as I'd ever seen. Either suited me.

"Down the far end." I nodded in that direction. "Just before my personal favorite number." I matched his smirk with one of my own. "Stick around after you finish and I'll show you why."

The kid stared at me until the meaning behind my offer sank in. He flushed scarlet, clutched the cart's handle and hurried off along the pathway more quickly than he'd arrived.

*Virgin, then, at least for the next couple of hours or so.* I tracked the line of his retreat. There was a certain unused peachiness about the arse he hid beneath faded jeans a couple of sizes too big. The rest of him was drowned in a green T-shirt with Garner Village Accommodation Cleaner emblazoned across the back. Sexy, though. Another potential notch if ever I'd clapped eyes on one.

"Seriously?"

I tore my attention from the boy's increasingly diminutive arse to Brian's raised eyebrows. "What?"

"Come on. You know what I'm talking about. That boy is sixteen if he's a day. And you think me checking out some twenty-year-old's tits is perverted."

"He's legal or he wouldn't be working here." And I didn't appreciate Brian implying otherwise. "Plus, there's a whole world of difference between your leering and mine. You're forty-fucking-eight. A quarter of a century older than me."

"I am not..." A dazed expression flitted across the folds of Brian's middle-aged face. Since the numbers would always add up to my total, he soon shook his head. "No matter the age difference, you're still a veteran compared to that boy. Don't you ever get into any bother with wrong signals?"

"Nope." Unlike Brian, I knew when I was flogging a dead horse. But with the way the kid tickled my chest with his lashes, I wasn't going to get into any trouble with him. "I only show 'em my dick. Up to them whether they want to sit on it." I squinted at Brian through a cloud of smoke. "Hadn't you better be getting back to work? Real work, I mean. Not drooling over the tits bouncing around in the outdoor pool."

"I'm on a break." Brian tapped my bare foot with his boot. "You could be doing something more productive than drooling over the new cleaning staff. Especially the ones whose balls have yet to drop."

"Do me a favor."

"A boss favor or a mate favor?"

"My van needs cleaning. Get the new member of staff down to do it."

"What's in that for me?"

I didn't have to think too hard. "Stacey's mate's number. I can get it for you." Stacey's mate wouldn't be best pleased, but that wasn't my problem.

"She's going home today. What good would that do me now?"

He had a point. I considered my options. "How about the next piece I hook up with, I put in a good word with her mate?"

"A hypothetical mate who could be a moose?"

I noted he didn't use the 'I don't cheat on my wife' line as a reason. "Fine." I reached into my jeans and pulled out a crumpled twenty. "This do you?"

"Nicely." He ferreted the cash away in his pocket.

I gathered up my phone and smokes, then rose from the lounger. "If anyone asks, I'll be out all afternoon. That way, I'll be a pleasant surprise for when the cleaning lad turns up."

Brian slowly shook his head. "It's like a home delivery service to you, isn't it?"

I paused on the steps to my van. "Mate, you sound almost, I don't know, jealous."

"Not of the fellas." Brian shook his head. "Still, your chances of getting this one pregnant are slim."

I lifted my hand and showcased my middle digit.

Brian ambled away, chuckling hard enough to set my teeth on edge.

# Chapter Two

I'd taken a quick shower, shaved and changed the sheets before my van door creaked open later that day. I settled back in my double bed and wondered how long it would take for the new boy to check out the master bedroom and find me waiting. I had a feeling this one might take more work than usual. The shy ones often did.

Naked with a semi tucked under the duvet, I tried to picture what he'd do when he did finally come in. He'd begin by playing hard to get. Nothing wrong with that. Just as long as he ended up under me at the end of it.

Right now, he was in the kitchen, making a noise with the few dishes I'd left out for washing. At least, I hoped it was him and the accommodation manager hadn't pulled a switch to put me in my place. The implications of having to chase one of the more overweight, not to mention odoriferous, members of the cleaning team from my van, while totally naked, hijacked my thoughts for a full half minute until the bedroom door pushed open and freed me from the nightmarish scenario.

There he was, loaded with an armful of bed linen, staring at me like I was an inflatable ten-foot cock rearing for the ceiling.

I ran a hand through my damp hair. No use pretending I hadn't been expecting him in the same way he hadn't been expecting me. "Don't mind me. You carry on."

The kid remained rooted to the spot. Just when I was beginning to think I'd got this all wrong, and that Brian was right about him being too young or too straight or generally too uptight, he spoke.

"I thought this caravan was empty."

I didn't have a type as far as men were concerned. I went for muscular and rough one day, sweet and pretty the next. Today was shaping up to be sweet and pretty, without a doubt. "My date cancelled. How old are you, kid?"

The kid straightened. "What's that got to do with anything?"

It had to do with the law and the fact that I had standards. "If you're over eighteen, it means I can offer you a beer."

"No, thanks." He wrinkled his nose. "My boss said if I came in here and found you in bed, I should run like hell."

I'd have to have a word with our accommodation manager. Slander, wasn't that the official term? "You know where the door is." I let the duvet slide south an inch, just to test the water.

"I'm nineteen." His gaze dropped to my exposed pubes. "Old enough to know what you're all about."

He dumped the linen at the end of the bed, then marched back through the bedroom door.

*Shit.* Blown it before I'd had a chance to blow him. I tossed the duvet aside and grabbed my underpants. I found him in the small kitchen packing his cleaning equipment away.

I leaned against the doorframe in nothing but a pair of briefs and a hastily arranged smile. "You going to pretend you're not all about the same?"

"I'm not about anything more than doing my job." He plucked a rubber glove from the worktop. "Which shouldn't involve standing here with a mostly naked person who hasn't even introduced himself yet."

"Dean." I took the hint. "You?"

"Peter. With an *i*."

"Like the bread?"

"Bread?"

"Pitta. Only, with an *r* instead of the…" What the hell was I blathering on about? Despite the fact that I was only half joking, because spelling wasn't my strong point and I didn't even get there was ever an *i* in Peter, he smiled. A forgiving smile. He had nice teeth, too, to complement his nice everything else.

"No. It's *P-i-e-t-e-r*."

"Oh yeah? What's your surname?" I asked, gently coaxing. "Pieper?"

Pieter rolled his eyes. "Croft." He finished packing his stuff, but rather than pick up the cleaning bucket and leave, he pressed his back to the worktop and folded his arms in a guarded but elegant parking position.

"Aren't you going to ask for mine?"

"I know yours, Dean Garner. And my boss told me I had to try and tolerate you the same as everyone else has to."

*I bet she has.* I'd have a bit of work to do here, putting him straight on a few things he may have heard down at Harridans' Haven, aka Housekeeping. "You fancy a coffee since you don't want beer?" I gestured to the top-of-the-range pod machine sitting proudly on my kitchen worktop. "It'll make whatever you want."

Pieter rested his hand on his hip, in the campest thing I'd seen him do, though he didn't seem the effeminate type. "And in exchange you expect me to make whatever you want?"

"I'll not deny it." Nothing wrong with a bit of honesty. Kid was a straightforward sort. Games wouldn't work with him as they did with Stacey, who was also sweet but, to be honest, boring.

"And you assumed I'd fall into bed with you because…" Pieter tapped his lower lip, which was, I noted, slightly plumper than the top. "Why, exactly?"

*Why is his bottom lip plumper than the top? No. Why do I think I could lure him into my bed? That's more like it.* "Because you gave me a look I recognized."

"What look?"

I stepped closer. "The look I imagine you wearing when you're riding my cock."

Once again, shock paled the kid's face. Or rather, faux shock, because I was willing to bet that was what it was.

He turned toward the door. "Forget the coffee."

"Hey! Don't go." I made to hurry after him, then stopped when I realized what he was doing. Not leaving. Just twisting the lock to make us nice and secure.

He swung back toward me, a sudden flash of color in his cheeks. "If this is going to happen, you'll do as I say." He took off his glasses and set them down on the kitchen counter. "Agreed?"

*Is he fucking with me?* I didn't mean in the good way. *Or maybe I do.* Because he was looking at me for an answer.

"Uh, agreed?" The word came out far more question than answer. If he was just taking the piss, the punchline had to come soon. Sooner than I would, anyway.

"Good." Pieter pulled his T-shirt over his head. His chest was pale, hairless. Hard though, too, not baby flesh. He had a glimpse of abs, definable enough to set my mouth to water. "I assume you have condoms. I've heard plenty about your reputation."

Okay. So maybe he was for real. That didn't mean to say he got to start taking liberties with my reputation. "You shouldn't believe everything you hear. Most of the staff are biased because I'm their bosses' son."

"Oh, I think they paint more than an adequate picture of what you're like." Piet tossed his shirt to one side. "But they haven't a clue what I'm like. Or what I like." He stepped close and cupped the bulge in my briefs. "Didn't I tell you to take these off?"

I wouldn't need telling a third time. When he let go, I shoved my underwear to my ankles. My hardening cock sprang free. "Like what you see?"

"I'm not sure." Pieter squinted at my dick. "I haven't got my glasses on."

*Cheeky fuck.* I kicked my pants to one side. "Come here."

Pieter's eyes remained scrunched up, but that made him even more delectable. I couldn't wait for him to wrap one of his fine-boned hands around my length and gauge the girth of me before I pushed up inside him. My dick lurched. Unless I wanted this over before it had begun, I was going to have to calm those kinds of thoughts right down.

I brushed my fingers along the ginger freckles scattered across his shoulder. His eyes were the most arresting shade of green and brown. Hazel, was that the color?

When I leaned in for a kiss, he turned his face aside. "I don't do that."

"What, kiss?"

"Not with you, no."

*What does that mean?* "I haven't got bad breath or anything." I blew a puff of air into his face.

Pieter wrinkled his nose. He pressed a cold palm to my belly and pushed. "Just get on the bed."

*Hold on.* Impatience was usually my thing. I took pride in taking charge. Women enjoyed it better that way, and blokes tended to follow my lead. I didn't recall anyone shoving me to the bedroom before. Or refusing to kiss me.

I stood my ground. We weren't done with this conversation. "About the no-kissing thing. Is that just with me?"

"Are you not on the bed yet?"

"You going to have any objections to me touching you?" I reached out with an aim to help free him from his jeans.

Pieter slapped my hand away. "I can undress myself, thank you."

"Then what can I do?" If he wasn't so fuckable, I'd have told him where he could shove his mid-morning shag.

"Get the condoms and the lube and lie on the bed." He puffed out an exasperated sigh. "Haven't we gone through this?"

*Right, so he likes to dish the orders. Does he also expect me to lie there and take it like a bitch, too?*

"I don't bottom." I blurted the words rather than saying them the way they sounded in my head. Quiet but firm.

"Now there's a revelation." Pieter opened his fly. "If it's confession time, I don't top. Which is why I'm here." His jeans dropped to his ankles. "Problem?"

I stared at his choice of underpants. "Are you a big *Sesame Street* fan?" I asked, assessing the gentle bulge distorting Elmo's face.

Pieter looked down. "Oh, those. They were a gift."

"From your mother?"

"No. From my…" His mouth hung open, full of an unfinished sentence. "Are we doing this or not?"

We were doing this, despite not being permitted to kiss or touch. *What I wouldn't give for a go on those pert nipples. Or a thorough exploration of his balls with my eager tongue.* Yeah, once we got going, I'd unwind that kid until he was pliant in my arms and crying out for more. I'd fuck every last nerve of uptight from his rigid body.

With that thought in mind, I made a slow stroll to my room and savored the kid's stare scalding my arse. I had a good arse. A fucking fantastic, tight-cheeked gem of an arse. I could tell without checking he was appreciating the view.

*He'll appreciate my cock soon enough, as well.*

# Chapter Three

Pieter sauntered in as I was rearranging myself on the bed. He strolled straight past me to the window, where he yanked the curtains closed. The room dimmed considerably, but I guessed that was his aim. His next move to was sweep his Elmo pants to his ankles.

Even with the newly subdued lighting and his hands clamped to his groin, I could tell only a semi stirred within that gorgeous thatch of strawberry-blond pubes.

"Everything okay?" I didn't get nervous when it came to fucking. But with this kid, I didn't have a clue.

"Yes." He focused on my cock. "Why aren't you wearing a condom?"

I tucked my hands behind my head. "I thought you might like to suit me up."

"Do you usually get other people to do your dirty work for you?"

"Is that how you see this?" If so, he should have run when he had the chance. There was nothing dirty about a spot of spontaneous sex. "Do you mind me asking why you're naked in my bedroom, looking like you're waiting for a circumcision with a rusty spoon and no anesthetic?"

Pieter swallowed. His hands dropped from his cock. "It's because I'm nervous. When I'm nervous I get defensive. And I need to—"

"Be in charge?"

"I don't like surprises."

Whether I liked surprises or not wasn't an issue, because this kid was full of them. *Surprises and issues.* "You can leave if you want. I've never forced myself on anyone, and I'm not about to start now."

"I'll let you know if I want to leave." He took a condom from the top of the bedside cabinet, then straddled my thighs, still no harder than before. I wanted to ask if he needed help, then decided to wait until he did the asking. And he would ask. Because everyone needed to be touched.

Pieter pinched the tip of the condom and rolled the latex over the head of my dick. His hands were cold and trembling. *Nerves or inexperience?* I couldn't tell. It didn't worry me either way, because, despite the chill of his touch and the uncomfortable silence, I stayed hard and wanting.

He squirted a ribbon of lube into one palm, then rubbed them together. His hands closed around my dick, coating my shaft in a thick, even layer.

"Looks like you're all set now." He withdrew too soon, and I mourned the fluttering motion of his labor-roughened hands. He rose over me and reached between his legs. Two lubed fingers forged a path inside his body just long enough for a slightly dazed expression to fall across his face.

I wished he'd allow me to open him up. That would have been difficult, if not impossible, what with this no-touching rule he had going on. This kid had taken charge and I didn't know how he'd react if I swept his illusion away.

When Pieter-with-an-i grabbed my cock, the warm pressure of his hand killed my breath. He rose on his knees, then shuffled forward until I was snug against his entrance. He bore down, teeth clenched, breath escaping in short puffs.

When I was in halfway in, he dropped forward. His slick body locked me between the fire of rampant arousal and the solid need for friction.

When he started moving, my dick pulsed in time to the roll of his hips. I clamped my hands to them before he had a chance to shove me away.

Pieter pushed his free hand to my belly, supporting himself as he bounced above me like a jaunty, not to mention pretty, car mascot.

"You enjoying yourself up there?" My breath was tighter than his arse, but the words had left my lips.

"Yes. Thank you." He dug his nails into my skin. "But I need…"

I tried to ignore the sting. "What?"

"I need more."

*More what? Cock?* "Without touching you?"

"Fuck me harder."

"Can we shift positions? With you under me, I can fuck you as hard as you like."

"No!" He let go of his shaft and moved both hands to my chest. "I need you to make me come."

*Way to state the obvious.* But if he wanted harder, I'd give him harder.

I firmed my grip and plunged deep. Pieter toppled forward. A shivery fire washed over me. I forged up inside him a second time with an equal amount of punch.

"God." He trembled between my palms. His cock leaked clear dew, a long streak of which had transferred to my belly, sheening my skin. "Yes. That."

I had a limitless supply of that. I thrust up, and this time Pieter held his balance. I must've struck gold, with the way he threw back his head and rode me.

We moved together, finding a rhythm, Pieter switching between stroking his dick and releasing to rebalance himself. Sweat dribbled from his chest to belly as he ground down, seeking his ecstasy as I sought mine.

My body ached with the passion of his need. Every scrape of his nails across my skin, every clench of his delicious arse, brought me closer. My balls throbbed with the urge to release.

Above me, Pieter slowed. He gripped his cock and worked it to a manic beat. His arse contracted, flooding my body with electricity. He uttered a single gasp. A long swathe of pearly cum splattered across my belly and chest.

Seeing the glaze of orgasm in his eyes, and, locked inside him, I released the pent-up passion I'd been clinging to.

The rush surged over me, thick as an inferno, powerfully scorching. When it was over, I sank into the mattress, letting the slow chill of the crash shiver over my skin.

# Chapter Four

When I came to again, Pieter was trying to pluck my fingers from his hips. After a moment or two's resistance, I relented and let him go. "You want to stick around a while?"

Pieter eased free, leaving my cock withering beneath the condom. He grabbed his Elmo pants from the floor and pulled them on. "I can't. I'm busy."

"Doing what?"

"What I do after work." He looked at me lounging boneless on the bed. "I should thank you, though."

"For the honor of scrubbing my van?"

"Hardly. I didn't exactly get around to it, did I?" A genuine smile tilted his lips. "I meant for the sex. Or is thanking you not appropriate?"

*Not so much inappropriate as weird.* I was getting used to Pieter's weird. "It's never happened before, but you can be the first." I patted the mattress. "Or you can show me your thanks instead."

Pieter glanced at my hand. "This isn't something I do often, and I don't want it to be awkward. It's best I go."

I propped myself up on my elbows. "Why does it have to be awkward? We could rest a few minutes and start over." He was the first person who'd interested me in quite a while.

"I'd rather not take the chance. I'll see you around the park, though. Possibly." He sauntered off as far as the kitchen to dress and pack up the rest of his cleaning gear. I could hear his bucket rattling from the bed.

I didn't go after him. I had no intention of filling the air with that kind of desperation. Pieter had it right. Leave before the awkwardness began.

I was dozing, snuggled in the earthiness of our session, when a light tap sounded at the door. After foraging my underpants from where I'd left them in the hall, I put them on and went to answer the door.

A vague silhouette filtered through the frosted glass. A trim figure in green. My heart surrendered a beat. Maybe he did fancy a second round after all.

When I opened the door to the girl I'd spent the last few hours trying to avoid, the fluttery sensation hardened to a rock that dropped straight to my belly.

I guessed by Stacey's exaggerated grin that she didn't feel the same. "I couldn't remember if you were coming to me or I was coming to you."

Considering I'd come for someone else already, and quite vigorously, I didn't feel like answering.

In the ensuing silence, Stacey's gaze slid to my chin. Then to my chest, belly and thighs. "Have you been sleeping?"

I raked a hand through my hair. "Yeah. I haven't been feeling well. Bit tired."

"What's wrong?" She climbed up a step. There were three leading up to my van. She'd started on the bottom. Now she was on the middle. "Do you need me to do anything for you?"

"No, I've got everything I need." Whatever it was we'd had was over. Why couldn't she sense that? She did nothing for me now. It wasn't her fault. It was what happened, and the main reason I was glad to live where I did. It meant every one of the girls — and boys — I spent the week with were gone by the following weekend. Then I could start afresh with someone new. *Perks of the job and a foolproof way to avoid a broken heart.* Or to appease a shattered one that could never be fixed.

"What happened?"

"Huh?"

Her fingers tickled across my abs. "Here."

I looked down to find Pieter's nail marks etched into my skin. "I don't know. Fleas?"

"In your bed?" She flashed enough teeth that she assumed I was joking. "There weren't any fleas when I was there." She forged over the threshold. "Either time."

Every step I took back, she claimed until my arse hit the kitchen worktop. Rarely did I regret the size of my van — it was more than large enough for one — but now was one of those times.

"What's that smell?" Stacy sniffed at my neck. "New aftershave?"

"I don't think so." I was wearing Eau de Mid-Afternoon Delight courtesy of the new and slightly eccentric cleaning boy. I'd have admitted that if it wasn't for the possibility of a smack in the eye. She could easily hook one out with her fake nails.

"I told Gabby I'd be fifteen minutes." She peered up at me. "So?"

"So?" I wasn't enough of a slut to swap bed partners within half an hour. Not with the sheets still warm from Pieter's presence.

She gave me a flirty laugh before heading straight for my bedroom.

"Wait!" I followed, too late for her not to catch the crumpled sheets and the bloated condom sitting on the bedside table.

"Oh." She blew the sound out in a breath.

I took in her stiff, tan shoulders under a green stringy top. "I can explain," I said, though there was nothing to explain. She and I weren't a couple. We'd enjoyed a brief summer fling, which had run its weeklong course. Time to move on now. For us both.

"You've been with someone else." It wasn't a question. "Who?"

"No one you'd know." I didn't care enough to attempt passing the condom off as the result of a quiet, mess-free wank with her on my mind.

"I don't know anyone here, do I?" She spun around to face me. "I thought you liked me. We swapped numbers and everything."

Numbers and body fluids, yet I'd condemned her to my expanding block-list. "I do." I softened my tone. "But I like other people, too. And this was never going anywhere, was it? You live like two hundred miles from here."

Stacey's lips twitched. "Who is she, another guest?"

"Does it matter? Don't you have a train to catch?" Cold, but I wanted rid. She'd got the message, so why wasn't she gone?

"Is this what you do?" Stacey lifted her chin. Her jaw trembled slightly, but she stood her ground. "You sleep with as many girls as possible? Like some sleazy Spanish waiter?"

"I never implied I was a saint."

"No. You're definitely more bastard than saint." Stacey remained defiant. She'd grown a pair somewhere between the van steps and here. "You said you didn't usually get involved with the guests because 'it wasn't professional'." She air-quoted the last word.

I'd never been professional in my life. I was full of shit. She was always going to find that out at some point, although I'd have preferred that time to be a week from now after I'd failed to make contact.

"He wasn't a guest," I said.

"He? As in a man?"

Pieter was more of a lad than an actual man, and I wasn't sure what she was picturing in her head, but judging by the revulsion twisting her lips, it wasn't anything good.

I wished this whole interrogation was over. "You could describe him as that."

"Are you telling me you're gay?"

*Assumptions. Everybody makes them.* I bit down on the bubble of anger ready to burst from my lips. "I don't wear labels and I don't restrict my options." When she flinched at my tone, I sighed. "Look, if it makes you feel any better, there's only been him since I met you."

"Doesn't he mean anything to you, either?" She fixed me with her sad blue eyes. If I said yes, would she feel any better? A no wouldn't do much for our situation, either.

"I don't know him." She deserved that much honesty. "Not beyond his name. He has a nice arse." I offered a comforting hand on her arm. She liked physical contact.

Now, she shoved me aside like I really was that sleazy waiter.

Stacey's face crumpled. "You said you'd call me every day. You said I could stay with you. You said — "

"I don't remember what I said." I grabbed my cigarettes from the bedside table.

She was right, though. I had said those things. Not because I meant them. Girls needed to hear that stuff. They liked to imagine what we were doing was more than just fucking.

I offered her a cigarette.

She stared at the pack without taking one. "You don't care anything about me at all, do you?"

Shit. She didn't smoke.

I fumbled a cigarette from the packet. "For the week we were together. But beyond that?" I bowed my head. *Shame?* I felt it. A touch. This was awkward, and nothing I'd choose to repeat. It was that Pieter kid's fault. Making himself so damn irresistible.

"All I can say is thank god you wore a condom. You're probably crawling with disease."

My nerves jangled to attention. "Why?" I tossed the cigarette packet at the bed. "Because sometimes I sleep with men?"

Stacey pulled her hands through her hair. "I'm not homophobic, you callous piece of shit! My cousin is gay."

"Yeah? Maybe you could introduce us sometime." As the steam spurted from Stacey's ears, I realized this was a bad time to be joking. Or was I joking? Stacey had good genes. If her cousin shared her golden hair and cupid lips, I wouldn't mind exploring what else they might have in common.

Her grief or anguish or misery—whatever the hell she'd been feeling—waned beneath the furious bloom flooding her cheeks. "He has better taste than to go with a completely disgusting sewer rat like you. You make me sick. I hate you. You're nothing but a...a man-whore." Her hand shot out, a blur until the solid weight of her palm struck my cheek. The hard smack of flesh on flesh bounced off the walls. The force of the slap made my molars ache. My cigarette tumbled from my fingers.

She tore past me, chased by her sobs. I didn't go after her. I didn't go after anyone. The smack hurt, though. Not physically, but just then I felt way more sewer-rat than man-whore.

I set about searching for my lost cigarette and found the stub smoldering under the bed, searing an ugly hole in the carpet.

# Chapter Five

By Monday morning, I'd almost got Stacey out of my head. I could say my slapped cheek stayed redder for longer than it took to forget her, but that wouldn't be strictly true. The look on her face when she discovered what a cheating bastard I was would stay with me for a bit longer. But the void where a conscience once resided had absorbed the pinprick of remorse that may or may not have burned through.

Still, as much as having been pronounced a disgusting sewer rat bothered me, the kid I'd fucked on Saturday afternoon bothered me more. Pieter Croft with an *i*. He hadn't been the best sex I'd ever had, but he'd been the first to thank me for it afterward. The quirkiness of our session had me curious to see where a second helping might take us. All I had to do was track him down.

I had Brian play detective on the cleaning rota. Turned out young Pieter had been reassigned to the other end of the park. By choice or design, who knew?

But it didn't take ten minutes to wander down by the vans lining the woods.

After skulking around the trees and peering through a window or two, à la Norman Bates minus the cross-dressing, I found him steadfastly vacuuming the lounge in two-o-five. He had his head down, but I recognized the unruly blades of tufty hair and the rounded curve of his arse as he turned his back to the window.

I stubbed out my half-smoked cigarette and made my way to the open door.

His jeans hugged his body, closer than the last pair I'd seen him in — and, come to think of it, out of. His arse jiggled with effort as he advanced the machine across the carpet. Was he wearing those Elmo pants again? With luck, I wouldn't have long to find out.

I strolled over to the power socket in the kitchen and pulled the plug.

The air stilled. Pieter returned to the vacuum and pummeled the start button a few times. His gaze flickered to the socket, from there to me with plug in hand. "What do you want?"

I had thought he'd be more appreciative of my company. Most of my conquests were, until my inevitable fall from grace. I hadn't had time to fall out of favor with Pieter, so his hostility was lost on me. "Just passing by. Thought I'd drop in to say hello."

"Hello." Pieter came over and snatched the plug from my hand. "And goodbye." He returned to the vacuum and busied himself winding in the cord.

"I'm not ready to leave yet." I wasn't sure why he was playing hard to get, but I had time enough to humor him.

"You can do what you want." Pieter picked up the vacuum in one hand and the hose in the other. "But I've still got work to do."

He started toward the open door. I crossed the kitchen at the speed of light and barred his way to freedom. "What's the hurry? Who cares if you take ten minutes off?"

"I've had my break."

"And I've had you, but that don't mean I can't come back for seconds."

Pieter dropped the vacuum. "If that was a chat-up line, you need to rethink your whole approach."

"It wasn't a line. It was a joke. A bad one, admittedly." More like a rancid one if his sour face was anything to go by.

"What do you want?" he asked for the second time.

"You don't need an answer, do you?" I inched a step closer. He smelled of dust, polish and a tang of sweat. He could reek like a warthog in a cesspit and it would have made no difference to me. Or my cock.

"You don't need me for that." A touch of nerves made his voice waver. He couldn't even meet my eye. "You could have anyone."

"I don't want just anyone." I risked further wrath by tucking a finger under his chin and lifting. "What happened to the glasses?"

His hand fluttered to his face. "I'm wearing contacts."

"Out to impress someone?" He needn't have bothered. I found him adorable with or without the glasses.

"No. It's easier to work with contacts. My glasses fall off every time I…" His breath hitched.

"Every time you what?" I imagined sliding into his body and the waves of pleasure awaiting me there.

"Every time I bend over." Pieter's lashes lowered. They were the same sandy hue as his hair and were long enough to cast a breeze with every dip.

"You haven't got a clue how hot you are, have you?" I forgot myself for a moment and leaned in to take a kiss.

When Pieter scuttled to the relative safety of the kitchen, I took the opportunity to close the van door. His actions were not those of a man wanting out but, rather, of one who needed the gentlest of persuasion to stay.

He stood with his back to the sink. His lower lip trembled, as though I'd launched an insult rather than a compliment. "I thought you would have forgotten about me."

"Why would I have forgotten you?" I drew closer. "You had fun, too. I can still feel your arse tighten around me as you came."

"God." Pieter stared so hard at his toes he might have been contemplating diving for cover in his shoes.

"No. I'm Dean, remember?" I didn't deserve the god title. Not until after we'd fucked again.

"I thought you would have moved on."

"To where?"

"To someone else. I've heard that's what you do, and I thought—"

I reached to stroke his freckled cheek. "Anyone ever mention you spend too much time thinking?"

Pieter threw out a palm to fend me off. "If we do this again, it's the same rules as before."

I lowered my hand. "Rules?"

"You don't need to kiss or touch me to have sex with me."

*Ah. Those rules.* "You don't need to hold your cock when you take a piss, neither. But it helps."

"In that case, you can hold your own cock and take a piss someplace else. I told you I have work to do."

When he made to move past me, I took his arm. "Do you always get to be in charge?"

"With you? Yes. You're practically out of control."

It took a lot to offend me, but Pieter Croft might just have managed it. "You've got a low opinion of someone you don't know."

"I don't have an opinion of you one way or the other." His lashes fluttered as he looked at me through them. How I didn't pin him down and tear the clothes from his body, I didn't know. Except it meant I wasn't so out of control after all.

"Bedroom." I gave him a shove in that direction. "Now!"

"Lock the door first." He tried to lunge past me. "Someone might come."

"Yeah, me. In you, with luck." No one would come in. They were all busy doing their work. That didn't stop Pieter battling me until I relented and secured the door, though.

When I returned, he had one foot in the bedroom, the other in the hall. "Are we done with the bullshit now?"

"I only asked you to lock the door," he said, full of haughty indignation.

I stepped past him into the bedroom and dived on the perfectly made-up bed. "I meant with the patronizing." I flipped over and settled into the pillows. "I get you think you're better than me, but we're in the same position here, aren't we?"

"What position?"

"This position." I toed off my shoes, then ripped my T-shirt over my head. "Are we doing this, or would you prefer to stand there while I get myself off?"

Pieter gave me the once-over, a dark fire igniting the depths of his pupils. "I like your body. You're toned."

I let him soak up as much of me as he desired. "Courtesy of the new gym off reception, if you're interested in beefing yourself up a bit."

"Are you saying I should?"

"Let's just get on with it, shall we?"

Pieter slipped out of his T-shirt. "Do you think I'm too skinny?"

"No. You're petite."

"For your information, I don't care what you think." He pushed his jeans to his ankles. "I don't have time to work out, anyway."

"What the fuck?" I focused on the orange blob with a beaming smile adorning his pants. "Mr. Tickle?"

"Yes." Pieter stuck out his hip. "Take them off me."

I sat up, eager to do his bidding. "What about the no-touching bee in your bonnet? Does that come off, too?"

"It's not a bee. It's a preference. Don't ask me to explain."

As if I would, when he wasn't forthcoming with any answers. His neurosis was cute for about five minutes, and we were about thirty seconds past that. I reached for the waistband of his pants.

His cock sprung free. This time he was halfway to hard and good enough to taste. I left his underpants hugging his thighs and clasped the base of his shaft.

Pieter grabbed my wrist. "I told you I don't want your hands on me."

"Don't worry, I'm not intending to use my hands." I leaned close and opened my mouth wide enough to indicate I meant business.

"No!" Pieter pushed both hands to my shoulders hard enough that his ragged nails dug into my skin. "Don't!"

I pulled back. "What the hell? I'm not going to bite it off."

"I don't want…nothing oral."

*Wow.* For a fraction of a second, he'd rendered me speechless. "This is the first time I've brought someone to tears before blowing them." Usually I'd be pissed to fuck, but there was something else with this kid. Rather than swipe him aside and forget him, it made my interest in him dig deeper.

"Can't we do the same as last time?" he said, all the strength ebbing from his voice. "If not, I'd rather not do anything."

Us not doing anything definitely wasn't an option. "Fine." I released my grip. "Same as last time it is."

# Chapter Six

I dug out condoms and lube from my pocket and set the lot on the bedside table.

Pieter studied the stash with a fair bit of disapproval. He picked up a sachet of lube and ripped the corner with his teeth. "Must be a slow week for eligible guests."

It wasn't slow. We were at the height of the season. Even had a few hen night parties in the bar of an evening. None had interested me enough to do more than serve the drinks and take their money. "I liked the first time enough to want a second."

Pieter climbed onto the bed and once again sat astride me. Being on top was clearly his favorite position. We'd have to work on that. "I hope you're not expecting me to moon after you like all your weeklong girlfriends do."

I wouldn't be averse to the possibility—not that I was going to let him know that. He wanted casual—that was what he'd get. "One more time, then it's like we never met."

"Exactly." When Pieter tugged at my fly, I decided to surrender control. It wasn't what I usually did in bed, but nothing about Pieter was usual. With my fly open and my belt undone, Pieter tugged at the waistband. "Lift up."

When I did so, he dragged my jeans and pants to my thighs then knelt on the bottom of the bed while he pulled off my shoes. With a bit of help from me, he soon had all my clothing on the floor.

My cock thickened this time without so much as a single caress. But no matter how desperate I might be to touch him, it wasn't worth the risk. I buried my hands under the pillow instead and hoped I could continue to resist temptation.

"You're quiet now you're hard." Pieter pressed his palm to the base of my cock. "Am I getting the silent treatment?"

I didn't answer. I figured I'd go where this no talking, no touching thing got us. I'd come for him no matter what he did. The mere memory of his orgasm hugging my cock like a long-lost lover would guarantee it.

Pieter grabbed a condom and the lube. He set both items down on my chest and released me to grease up his fingers.

The chill of the lube cut through my arousal. "You might've warmed it."

"We don't have time for that kind of luxury." Pieter swapped the lube for the condom. "I've got another three vans to clean after this one. Plus, I'll have to change the bedding in here again." He broke open the condom and slipped the latex deftly over my dick.

"Don't worry." I thrust into his fist. "I'll help you clean."

"I'm sure you will." He smothered his fingers in more lube, then slid a couple of digits between his legs.

"I could help you there, too." I focused on his arse sucking in those fingers to the second knuckle, knowing soon enough I'd be buried in that same heat.

"You should go back to not...talking." His thighs tensed. His cock stood to his belly. Three fingers inside now, and the condom was getting more constricting by the second.

As much as he was enjoying himself, I ached to be inside him. It took every gram of willpower I owned to keep my hands tucked out of the way under the fucking pillow.

"You said we didn't have much time?" My breathiness betrayed how horny I was for him, but I couldn't keep my mouth shut forever.

"I rushed this the last time. I want to be ready for you." He sounded just as breathy, and if he delved any deeper, he'd be wearing himself as a glove puppet.

My hands clenched under the pillow. "You're fucking with me now."

"Not yet." Pieter pulled out, then wrapped the same hand around my cock. The heat residue from inside his body seared through the condom. A shuddery thrill raced down my spine, shocking my hips into thrusting.

I grasped the pillow. "You are gonna kill me."

"Can it wait until after I've come?" Pieter shuffled forward until his body was directly over my cock. "We've wasted enough time as it is."

*Whose fault's that?* I might've asked, but, when his hand folded around my cock and lined me up with his delicious arse, I lost my breath.

I sank in a good inch before any real resistance hit.

Pieter bit his top teeth down on his lower lip. His breath came in short, sharp punches.

The need for friction itched across my skin. If I had my way, I'd flip us over and pound him clean through the mattress. Only there was an unwritten rule. We did things Pieter's way or not at all. That was the reason I kept my mouth shut and my hands under the pillow.

There was quite a bit wrong there.

"Are you okay?"

I opened my eyes, not realizing until now that I'd had them closed. Pieter's face shimmered into view.

"Yeah. Why?"

"You look angry. What are you thinking?"

*What does it matter? We're here to fuck, aren't we?* "I'm thinking time's ticking."

Pieter shifted his hands to my chest. "Do you have somewhere else to be as well?" He rolled his hips. The silky warmth inside him massaged my cock and sent a jolt of arousal to my balls.

I gritted my teeth. "You wanted this quick."

"But not that quick. I like the feel of you inside me. You're very filling."

"Like a double Big Mac?" My darkening mood sparked with glimmers of light. Resenting him wasn't going to win me any prizes. And I had a feeling Pieter was way better at sex when he was in a good mood rather than a bad one.

His arse clamped tighter. "With extra-large fries on the side."

I sucked in a breath. "Pieter, please." I wasn't begging, but it was a close call. My balls throbbed. My hands were threatening to detach from my wrists and grope their way to his body.

"Time me."

"Time you doing w — Fuck!"

Pieter slammed down. The headboard rattled. His arse slapped my thighs. Arousal cascaded through me, drawing out a low groan from the depths of my belly. He didn't give me a chance to catch a breath before he surged up on his knees. Cool air whispered over my damp shaft. He drew back right to the head before thumping down, swallowing me hard.

His fingertips slid over my nipples. He pinched the tips with a tweak I didn't have time to process before he was up and crashing down again, leaning over me, grinding down, clearly chasing his release with fuck all thought as to how I might be going on.

Pieter's backside slapped against my thighs. His breath puffed from his lungs in short, concentrated bursts.

I could see my cock, inch after inch exposed, before Pieter swallowed me again. Locked inside a torrent of heat. The tension-built wall upon wall with nowhere to go.

When I raised my gaze, Pieter's was focused somewhere above the headboard.

It was as though I wasn't even there, and he was using me to get off. The realization wasn't entirely unappealing, but I didn't want to be his sex toy. I wanted the connection.

"Hey." I found my voice from somewhere, thin and broken with the vibration of Pieter's pounding. His roughened palms skittered to my ribs. His nails bit into my skin, but if there was pain, I didn't feel any.

"Almost…almost…" He snatched one hand from my chest and grabbed his cock. He pumped himself, hard and firm, riding me like he was a fucking rodeo star. *Fuck me, he'd look good in a Stetson.*

I might've told him if he hadn't frozen solid after slamming himself down. He shivered and let out a low groan. His arse contracted, massaging me as effectively as the fist he had wrapped around his cock.

He came with a low growl and a thick stream of cum. When he was done, he sagged, pushing both hands up my belly, spreading cum over my skin. "You're not done yet?"

"Nope." I nudged into him, keeping the rhythm going but at a far slower rate than before. "Nope. Look at me."

"Why?"

Because it beat having him staring off into space, trying to picture me as someone else. I bit my tongue. Now wouldn't be the finest time to voice my observation. Not unless I wanted to spend the rest of the day with blue balls.

"It'll help," I said. Something else would help, too. I slipped my hands out from under the pillow and slid them along his smooth thighs.

"Okay," he said warily, but he didn't slap my touch away. He lifted himself, gradually, then rocked down. The fury had gone and he was languid in his exhaustion. "Is this good for you?"

"I prefer slow." Slow offered a chance to study him, because he was intriguing as fuck.

"I don't have time for slow."

Whereas I had all day, so tough tits. This was going to take as long as it took and not a second shorter. "If you tense up, then I tense up. And I can't come if I'm tense."

"The question is, are you going to come at all?" He tilted forward, leaning on his hands, and dipped close enough that his breath tickled my neck and chin. "I'm getting sore."

"Good. I like to leave a lasting impression." I cupped the warm cheeks of his arse. "A kiss might help. Just one. I'm not greedy."

"Not. A. Chance."

I found his rhythm again, savoring the pressure building inside me. The heady pull of approaching release surged over me, cock buried deep, my hips rearing off the mattress. My climax tinted the world in white.

Pieter was up and off me before my last orgasmic shudder had tripped through my body. As I lay there, all wilting dick and saggy condom, he was grabbing his clothes off the floor and putting them on, while I had yet to recover full feeling in my extremities.

"Why're you always in such a hurry?" I slurred, fighting to keep my eyes open. I could quite easily kip the rest of the morning, and I'd sooner do that with a warm body next to me.

"These vans don't clean themselves." Pieter pulled his T-shirt over his head. "I'm hoping to finish early today."

"I told you I'd help. Just let me get my breath first." I lazily patted the mattress. "Give me some CPR to help out."

Pieter paused to look at me. He stood way down at the end of the bed, hands on his hips, fully dressed now and ready to go. "Haven't you got bored of me yet?"

"I only wish I had."

His brow lowered. "Why?"

"Because my foreseeable is going to involve a lot of unnecessary hide and seek." I lifted my head. "Unless you want to leave a note of where you'll be any given day."

"That would be too easy. Besides, didn't we agree this wasn't going to happen again?"

Had we? I couldn't remember. But even if we had, I wasn't going to abide by that rule any more than he was. Otherwise, why mention anything about not making this easy?

"Whatever you say." I rested my head back on the pillow. "Won't happen again." Until the next time. I kept that last part to myself, but I heard those exact words buzzing around Pieter's head as he left.

# Chapter Seven

"You are a difficult man to please." Pieter frowned down at me as if I'd drawn the sex out on purpose. Which I may well have done, to keep him here a little longer. If only physically, because his mind was somewhere else when we were together. His eyes held that same distant focus and I could never fuck him hard enough to catch up.

It had become a bit of a thing, running into him in various vans around the park. Or rather, the beds located within the vans around the park. I'd even taken to carting about an extra set of linen to replace what we used, which I think he appreciated because it saved explaining why he always seemed to be short of the correct amount.

After lighting up a cigarette, I settled into the pillow and waited for him to decide what he was going to do. I was surprised he hadn't dismounted and dressed, considering his usual eagerness to get away.

This time, though, when he climbed off, it was only to sink into the other pillow. "Have you got one of those for me?"

"You smoke?" He seemed too clean, too conservative for such a vice, despite the sex.

"Weed, mostly. But I'm assuming you don't have any on you."

I couldn't work out if he was joking or not. He didn't crack a smile, so I assumed not. I offered him my cigarette, cupping the red end in my palm. "It's my last one."

"I'll save you some." He pinched the filter before drawing it to his lips and taking a deep drag. "I haven't had one of these in ages."

"Here." I passed him the empty pack to use as an ashtray.

We lay together, naked on top of the mattress, comfortably relaxed. My cock ached from the pressure of his body. His arse had to be chafing, too. But this was the first time he'd lain with me afterward and I was going to savor every moment.

"Why are you working here as a barman?" he asked, after a while of doing nothing but smoke and listen to the birds in the trees. "Don't your parents want you to take over as boss once they retire?"

*That'll be the day. They'd rather go bankrupt first.* I daresay they would go bankrupt if I had any say in the way this place was run. "Nope."

"Don't you want to? The manager here must make a lot more than you do."

"Money doesn't interest me. Why you asking?"

"Don't worry, I'm not seeking a sugar daddy. Just interested."

*Sugar daddy? What the...* "You're only three years younger than me."

"Yes, but I'm in a whole other decade."

He was also a smart-arse who needed the equally smart smirk wiped off his face. I grabbed the cigarette back off him and let the comment go. Fucking Pieter was a whole lot more interesting than arguing with him.

"I'm not going to inherit nothing," I said with complete certainty. The lot would go to my business-savvy older sister. I'd always known my folks favored her as heir, even before my relationship with them had drawn to an abrupt halt. "In case you hadn't noticed, I'm too self-absorbed." My dad's words echoed around my head every now and then, along with other, less complementary phrases. "I'm more mechanic than managing director material, anyway."

"There's nothing wrong in being a mechanic." Pieter rolled toward me and propped his head in his hand. I could sense him staring at me, probably running a whole list of questions through his brain. He settled for, "How long have you been living here?"

"This time around? A couple of years."

"What do you mean, this time around?"

I didn't know why I'd said that. By doing so I'd unwittingly opened up another area of my past I wasn't willing to talk about. "Just that I've lived here a few times over the years. It's been a good place to keep my head down."

"From what?"

From a whole bunch of things I still wasn't prepared to talk about. Not to him, or anyone. "From my parents. After I quit school before my A-levels. It wasn't what my parents had planned for me." There were a lot of things my parents hadn't planned for, including my birth. Which I had a knack of reminding them about whenever I proved their disappointment in me was warranted.

"Then what did you do?"

"I traveled. Worked in a few bars around Europe. Now I'm here, vegetating while I decide how to waste the rest of my life."

"I don't think you've wasted anything." He plucked the cigarette from my fingers and took a long toke before handing it back. "Your life has been more exciting than mine. I've never even been abroad."

"Why not?"

"Because I could never afford it." He sat up, too quickly. "Speaking of which, I'd better get back to work." He grabbed a pillow and divested it of its case. "Here. You'd better clean yourself up."

I stared at the case in his hand. "You made the mess. I reckon you should do the honors."

"Of course you do." He might've even flashed me a smile before he stroked the pillowcase across my cum-soaked belly.

I let him continue until he was done, then pushed ahead with what I'd been planning to ask for a while now but could never quite find the right time. "How do you feel about taking this beyond the bedroom?"

"You mean outside?" Pieter balled the pillowcase up in his hand. "With the possibility of someone seeing us?"

I had to clear my throat to cover a laugh. *And I thought the way I'd asked him was designed to ease his bashfulness.* "No. I'm not looking to give any potential voyeurs a free show. What I meant was, maybe we could go for a drink. Or dinner." Dinner? Had I just asked him out for fucking dinner? If anything, he looked more shocked by that than the idea of al fresco sex.

"Why?"

I thought he'd respond a bit more enthusiastically. "Why not?"

"Because this is just for sex, isn't it? Going for a drink would make it something else."

"And?"

"And I don't think..." He looked towards the bedroom door. "What was that?"

I sat up, irritated by the interruption, the unnecessary change of subject. "What was what?" Just as I spoke, the van floor shuddered.

"Hello?" a female voice called. "Pieter?"

"Shit!" Pieter leaped off the bed and disappeared, taking the duvet with him and leaving me exposed to the world.

The bedroom door opened.

A chubby blonde appeared in the doorway in a black T-shirt stretched over her many bulges. Her gaze met my cock. "I was, um...looking for someone called Peter."

"With an *I*?" I got up, clutching my jeans to my belly, hoping the legs would adequately cover my 'nads.

The girl's mouth hung open. "S-sorry?"

"He's over there." I gestured in the vague direction Pieter had disappeared in.

The girl's face throbbed scarlet. "I was told to give him this." She tossed something onto the bed. A key. "It's for another van that needs..." A manic giggle burst from her lips. "...seeing to." She clapped her hand over her mouth and made a dash for the door. The van rocked with her thunderous retreat.

"Anyone would think she'd never seen a naked bloke before." I shot a glance at Pieter. Or rather at the top of his sandy head, because his face was pressed into the side of the mattress. "What's wrong with you?"

Pieter looked up. His cheeks lit with enough fire to sear the mattress down to the springs. "What do you think is wrong with me?"

"You hurt yourself when you fell off the bed?"

He brushed his hand across his eyes. "Fuck you."

"Thanks. But you've already had the privilege." I pulled on my jeans. "Is this about our visitor? Don't think she saw your dick if that's what's bothering you." In fact, I doubted she'd even seen him. I grabbed the key she'd thrown on the bed. "You got four vans to do now. We'd best get started."

Pieter hadn't moved from his cubby-hole between the mattress and the wall.

"This is about what happened?" I hadn't realized. Mostly because I'd given up caring what other people thought about me, staff or anyone else-wise. "She won't say anything. I can make sure of it."

"How?" Pieter's tears were fat enough to roll down both cheeks. Tears got me, every time, female or male, although, I had to admit, no bloke had ever cried in front of me before. Except Brian a time or two, when he'd had another row with the wife and stayed over in my spare room.

"Give me a moment." I grabbed my T-shirt off the floor. "I'll go and have a word." I stepped into my shoes, then headed to the door. I held back for some gratitude. None came.

Pieter remained a puddle of embarrassment on the floor. He was as queer as a strawberry Skittle, but his curled spine told me he'd as soon have suffocated himself in the mattress than have anyone beyond this van know it.

A heavy gloom accompanied me from the van and into the sunshine. I barely knew the kid, but I enjoyed his aura of uncertainty mixed with his determination to get what he wanted. There wasn't much evidence of control or determination about him now. His spark had drowned in the cold bucket of shame he was currently wallowing in.

I dealt with the girl before she reached gossip central. By the time I left her, she'd got the message. Pieter's virtue was safe, and she'd not say a word. Not if she valued her job. I didn't have any pull with management, but there was no need for her to know that.

I returned to the van to give Pieter the good news. Only, he wasn't there. Neither was his cleaning stuff. Or his clothes, come to that. Nothing of him remained except various body fluids on the sheets and a pair of well-worn Scooby Doo underpants staring up at me from the bedroom floor.

# Chapter Eight

I didn't go out of my way to track him down, not after the way he'd behaved. But I remade the double bed with the linen I'd brought for the occasion and cleaned the vans he still had left to do that day. I considered that apology enough, although I wasn't sure I had anything to apologize for beyond forgetting to lock the van door.

The kid was totally in the closet. Had to be, with that kind of extreme reaction to getting caught out. I tried to convince myself that things ending this way was for the best. I didn't do romance anyway, let alone relationships. Not that I intended to have a relationship with Pieter. The look of horror on his face when I suggested we go for dinner was confirmation enough that he felt the same way.

But I couldn't help but think it was all such a waste. Him and me, we could have had something together. Indefinite hot sex. Even on a monogamous basis, if he insisted. It wasn't like I had anyone else on the radar.

I was on a break from an afternoon shift at the clubhouse when Brian ambled over and took a seat at the bar.

"What's up with you?"

"How'd you mean?"

"I mean with your sudden lack of female company."

That he clearly hadn't heard about what had gone on in van one-fifty meant that the cleaning girl had taken me at my word. I was almost impressed by her ability to keep that particular golden nugget a secret.

"I dunno. Nothing." I fetched us both a coffee. "I might be seeing someone later." I was going to track Pieter down at the park, and get the other afternoon sorted out. We weren't done yet, not by a long shot.

"One of them?" Brian nodded toward the windows. A gaggle of girls sat at a table with their full English breakfasts. I'd taken their order earlier and flirted as much as my disinterest would allow.

When a couple of them looked back, Brian presented one of his try-hard smiles. "Which one will be warming your bed tonight? I'll wager the brunette. Though the redhead has got a jubbalicious set of..." He angled his palms toward his flabby chest and made squeezing gestures with his fingers.

"Have you seen Pieter lately?"

Brian's grin vanished. He lowered his hands. "Who?"

"The kid who's been cleaning my van." I tried to sound nonchalant, despite the mere mention of him churning my guts. "Looks a bit like the bastard offspring of Ron Weasley and Harry Potter."

"The jailbait? Why'd you want to know?" His question made it clear the park grapevine wasn't as fined-tuned as Pieter believed it to be. "Don't tell me you're humping it?" When I lifted a shoulder, he blew out a breath. "You are, aren't you?"

I'd done nothing but focus on the girls by the window to give more credence to my denial. "No." I tapped the side of my head. "Faulty gaydar."

"Don't suppose it matters now, anyway." Brian took a deep gulp of coffee. "Way I heard it, that lad quit a week ago."

* * * *

Getting Pieter's address didn't take more than a basic ten-minute charm offensive on the new girl at reception. That and a solemn promise I wasn't up to no good got me what I wanted via the mail outbox, which, I was reliably informed, contained a P45 bearing Pieter's name and address. He wasn't just a Croft, either. He was a Winterson-Croft. Double-barreled and quite the mouthful. Not that I'd ever put his mouthful to the test, being as he was allergic to anything oral.

Pieter lived in a smart block of flats on the outskirts of the town center, a five-story red-bricked building with modern bay windows. I found a parking space outside the block then made my way to the main door.

Flat Four on the intercom had the name Winterson handwritten beside the button. No Croft, but there wasn't enough room for the essay of Pieter's name on the tag.

I hit the buzzer. No answer. I rang again, this time with a backup plan. I'd wait until someone was coming in or out, get into the building and sit in the corridor until he either came home or actually answered the door.

"Yes?" The voice burst from the speaker so suddenly I almost flinched. "Who is this?"

*Good question.* I wanted to ask him the same, since he clearly wasn't Pieter and I hadn't been expecting anyone else. "Uh, I'm looking for Pieter Croft."

The intercom crackled. "You obviously didn't understand the question, so I'll rephrase. Who are you?"

*Sarky fucker.* I had no idea who this loser was, but I decided there and then I didn't like him. "Me and Pieter…" *Me and Pieter, what?* Pieter wouldn't thank me for outing him, especially as this guy could be an oblivious flatmate. "We work together."

"Dean? Why didn't you say so?"

The door buzzed open.

*Has Pieter told him about me?* He must've said something, since my name had served as a key. And without me having to give it to him. Did this mean Pieter wasn't so far back in the closet as I'd assumed? The idea warmed me considerably. Pieter had told someone about me? *Us.* In what capacity, I didn't know. But it had been enough to get me entry, so it couldn't have been all bad. It meant I wasn't such a nonentity with him after all.

Flat Four was the last door on the right down a length of bright, clean hallway. I gave the door a jaunty tap, but it took a few moments for it to open.

The guy on the other side bore no resemblance to the gruff, sarcastic loser I'd envisioned on the other end of the intercom. His powerfully green eyes bored into mine. When he didn't so much as blink, I let my own gaze roam to his generous mouth, made to look all the more generous by a jaw sharp enough that, if not for the faint mossy growth of stubble, I'd have mistaken him for a girl.

"Yes?" He spoke the word in a lazy drawl, like I was boring him when I'd yet to say a word.

I made another decision not to like him. Or the symmetrical perfection of his features. Or his weird violet-silver hair as fine as silk thread. Or the way I couldn't stop staring in the hope of discovering a flaw.

"Are you going to speak? If not, you should close your mouth before something flies in."

My jaw snapped shut. My brain scrambled for something — anything — to say. "Is Pieter home?"

"No."

"Do you know when he's due back?"

The lad's bony shoulder shifted under a too-big shirt. "He went to collect a prescription."

A prescription? Was he ill? I wanted to ask, but this guy unnerved me. "Maybe I should come back later."

"No. He won't be long. You can come in." The kid pulled open the door.

For the first time, I got a full view of the ghostly wraith before me. Slimmer than Pieter, his clothing drowned him. An oversized checked shirt over a thin vest and faded jeans billowing around his legs. His feet were encased in a pair of fluffy cat-shaped slippers. It was as if he'd had a fight with a jumble sale stall and lost.

I hesitated before entering, mainly because my feet itched to hurry away. I had no real reason to be here, except for Pieter's P45 and his unwashed Scooby underpants burning a hole in my pocket. I could hand those over. *Okay, maybe not the pants, but…sod it.*

I stepped inside.

The air inside was hot as an old folks' home, and it was a heat that only intensified as I followed the lad down the hall and into a small, cluttered lounge.

"Take a seat." He lurched past me to half-sit, half-collapse into an old brown sofa.

"Are you okay?" I asked, because he was very pale and looked as if he might pass out.

"Yes." The kid rested his head back into the cushion. "I've been busy."

I found myself studying the lines and angles of his features and wondering how he managed to hold on to his beauty. Because he was quite exquisite. From his violet hair to his arched eyebrows. It was creepy to stare, but I carried on doing it until a quiet voice inside my head suggested I was beginning to resemble Brian slathering at the women through the slats in the fence lining the outdoor pool.

I shifted my focus to the art on the wall. An embroidered cat behind a thick glass frame. A painted country cottage with roses around the door. All very homey. All very middle-aged. A wooden bookshelf dominated one corner, filled with colored glass ornaments and tiny pewter dragons in neat orderly rows. At the other end of the room, a small kitchenette contained a pristine worktop and a shiny kettle on a hob.

Beyond the chair was a set of French doors leading on to a small paved patio. There were plants out there. Filled pots and a wooden picnic bench. Cute space for a smoke, and I'd have killed for a cigarette just then.

I took a chair with wooden arms directly across from the fireplace. Despite this being August and naturally warm outside, all three of the electric bars glowed orange.

"My name is Nix," he said, in such a way I half-expected him to add 'and I'm an alcoholic'.

I didn't need to tell him mine, since he knew it. Courtesy of Pieter, which lent me the hope that all was not lost on that score.

"It's short for Phoenix." He gave me a level stare, as if seeking out a barely stifled laugh. He wouldn't get one from me, but who lumbered their kid with a name like Phoenix? Cute now, not so much as a balding fifty-year-old with a flatulence problem. "Why are you here?"

Kid was kind of blunt, but I reached into my jacket and plucked the envelope free of the pocket. Unfortunately, I dislodged the underpants and a startled-if-creased Scooby now stared up at me from a threadbare purple rug.

"Oh, Piet thought he'd lost those."

The air began to smolder. There was no way I could explain them without admitting to the truth. Still, I could try. "He left them. At work. By...accident."

"You could have kept them as a souvenir. He wouldn't have minded."

*A souvenir? Jesus!* "What has Piet told you about me?"

"He said your technique could use some fine-tuning."

"My technique?"

"Yes. Would you like some tea? I've boiled the kettle."

My throat locked. I couldn't answer. All I could do was watch him struggle out of the sofa and inch across the floor. A kid younger than me, hunched over, face flat in pained concentration. A kid who knew all about me and Pieter. In detail. Nix reached the kettle and paused, both hands clinging to the worktop. "Breakfast...or green?"

"Sorry?"

"Tea. Which do you prefer."

Neither, but I was too in shock to risk conversation. I wanted to grab this scrap of weirdness by his paper shoulders and shake everything Pieter had ever said about me out of him. "I dunno. Whatever. What did Piet mean about fine tuning?"

"He said you're too submissive." Nix pulled open a cupboard and took out two cups. "But don't worry. You'll soon learn. Next time you—"

"Next time? What makes you think there will be a next time?" Before this, I would have done anything to secure a next time. But that was before I found out Pieter had been discussing my sexual techniques with all and sundry.

"Because you're here." He looked over his shoulder. "You haven't answered my question."

"What question?"

"Breakfast or green?" He held up a box. Green tea. My taste buds shuddered.

"Breakfast. One sugar."

"Ah, you're working on your assertiveness already. Piet will be pleased."

I thought it best not to respond. Every time I opened my mouth, something worse came out of his.

"Do you mind?" Nix said after a few minutes of stifling silence. He gestured to the brimming mugs. "I don't trust myself not to spill any."

"So, um, what did you do?" I got up and crossed the few feet into the kitchen area. "To your leg." If I could keep the topic of conversation on him, it couldn't possibly work itself around to me and my performance in bed again. Could it?

"Nothing. It's my muscles."

"Your leg muscles?"

"No. All of them."

As I moved closer, his scent swirled the air. Soap and menthol. Beneath those two strong aromas, something murkier. Sickness. Not born of any physical injury. He exuded the musty, sickly-sweet perfume no hospital disinfectant could mask.

"But I'm not dying. It isn't terminal."

"I never said…" Sometimes it was best all round to let a subject drop. I picked up both mugs. "Let's go and drink these teas before they get cold, shall we?"

"Piet will have gone for a coffee," Nix said on our return to the lounge. "He does that, when he needs a break."

"A break from what?"

"Me. Of course."

I looked away before he could tell I'd guessed the answer. There was something wrong with this kid, besides the physical issue. I daresay anyone would want some freedom from this level of honesty every now and then.

I set both mugs down on a side table. "Is that what Pieter does? He takes care of you?"

"Yes. He's my best friend."

Now we were getting somewhere. Best mates sharing a flat. Only Pieter had been landed with the raw deal if he spent most of his time as a live-in carer.

I retook my seat. "How long have you two been living here?"

"Three years. We…" Somewhere beyond the open door leading to the hallway, a lock disengaged. "Oh, Piet's back."

Nix pushed himself out of his chair and edged a painful path into the hall, still wearing those ridiculous cat slippers.

"What are you doing?" Pieter's voice flamed into the room from beyond the door. "Where's your stick?"

"You've got a guest," Nix said, his breath coming in hard.

"Who?" Wariness replaced Pieter's alarm. I looked around for somewhere to set down my tea, then decided to keep it and look relaxed, ready to see him. "What?"

I hadn't heard Nix say my name. He must have whispered it, like I was a demon or something. And judging by his tone, that was exactly what Pieter thought I was, too.

He stormed through the door a moment later, wielding a carrier bag whose contents rattled when he dropped it at his feet. "How the hell did you find out where I live?"

I took a sip of tea and settled into the chair. His P45 lay in my lap, but I wasn't ready to present him with it yet. "Good to see you as well."

"That isn't an answer." Pieter's hands clenched to fists at his sides. He had on a natty fitted red wool jacket and a pair of smart dark denim jeans. Kid looked just as steamy as his temper.

"I don't understand why you're not pleased." Nix limped back into the room. "Dean's been keeping me entertained."

"You have the TV and your iPod for that. You shouldn't have answered the door."

I snorted into my tea, then found myself the subject of Pieter's flame-filled attention once again.

"What?"

"Come on." I gestured to Nix. "You're treating him like he's your kid rather than your flatmate."

"Flatmate?" Pieter was now as rigid as my cock had been when I had him bang to rights in my bedroom. "Who told you he was my flatmate?"

I switched my attention to Nix. "Him. He said you were best mates. I assumed—"

"Are you blind?" Pieter gestured to the wall behind him.

I scanned the blank space above the electric fire. "What am I meant to be looking at?"

Pieter spun around. "Where is it?"

"Where's what?" There was a nail up there. Above a rectangular patched of wallpaper lighter than the rest.

"Our picture, Phoenix?"

Nix wilted under the pressure of Pieter's fierce gaze. "I put it in the bedroom," he said, speaking so quiet I barely heard him. "I thought it might complicate things."

"Complicate what?" I was done with the whole listening thing. It wasn't getting me any further out of the darkness. Everything this pair said contained English words but was spoken in a combination foreign to me. "What don't I know?"

"I told you that was all just talk," Pieter said, totally ignoring me. "He's not suitable. Not for me. And not for us."

"But he is." Nix grabbed Pieter's arm. "He doesn't care about anyone but himself, which means he won't get too attached. You can train him to be better at sex, and—"

"What the fuck!" I leaped up from the chair, spilling the tea down my thighs and the P45 on to the floor. I slammed the mug down on the side table. "Are you still talking about me?"

"Yes." Nix blinked at me. "Why are you shouting?"

I drew myself up, as if an inch on my height would make me any more thoughtful. Or significant. "You don't know me. You can't go about making those kinds of wild judgments." Setting aside the bad-sex accusation for one moment. "I do care about people. I care plenty."

Pieter swiped up the carrier bag from the floor. "You care about yourself. I don't see you making any effort to include anyone else on that list. Nix, sit down before you fall. I'm going to put this lot away." He stalked off into the kitchen, then pulled boxes of pills from the bag and stuffed them into a cupboard that looked to contain a good few pharmaceuticals already.

"Why do you keep banging on about my sexual technique?" I jabbed a finger at Nix's chest, stopping just shy of touching, lest he shatter. "I've never had complaints. I've especially had no complaints over someone I haven't even had yet."

"Yet? Oh. I'm not a part of the arrangement." Nix shrank back from my finger. "Piet didn't tell you I was, did he?"

"Arrangement?" I looked to Pieter for enlightenment. Some hope.

"You know I wouldn't do that." Pieter shouldered past me. He disappeared into the hall and came back with two things. One of them was a pink walking stick adorned with purple ribbons, which he handed to Nix. "Use this. You don't need to impress anyone, least of all him."

He marched to the fireplace and hefted the second thing he'd carried in and hung it from the nail in the wall. "See?" Pieter said, his voice sounding strained. "Not my flatmate."

I followed the line of his finger to the canvas now sitting above the fireplace.

It was an image of the two of them in matching light grey suits and cream ties. Pieter grinned with pride from in his too-big glasses, and Nix wilted against him, beautifully enigmatic in a photogenic can't-take-my-eyes-off-him way. He had a glass of champagne raised to the camera. No. It couldn't have been alcohol because he didn't look more than twelve there. But their ages weren't the thing that distracted me the most. That honor belonged to the 'Just Married' caption in black fancy calligraphy through the center of the canvas.

"Come on," I said more to myself than them. "This is a joke, right?"

"Not a joke." Pieter moved in front of the canvas. "And you're wasting your time here. There's bound to be richer pickings at your park to keep you entertained."

"That's no wedding photo. You look like two kids at a LGBT school prom."

"We were sixteen. Hardly kids."

*Sixteen? They were exactly kids.* This had to be a sick prank. "Is that legal?"

"With parental consent, which we've always had."

*What parent would agree to their kids marrying at sixteen?* Straight marriages were hard enough, but considering the 'phobes out there, they must've had a lot to contend with. In another life, I'd have admired their bravery. Instead, I felt flat. No. Worse. Betrayed.

"You're his husband." I turned to Nix, who was curled up on the sofa casual as a Sunday afternoon.

"Me and your significant other have been fucking for weeks. I had plans to do him in every van in the park and that doesn't bother you?"

"Why should it?" Nix regarded me skeptically. "Piet needs sex. And I don't."

"You mean you can't fuck because you're not up to it, so you send your husband off to get it elsewhere?" I spun to face Pieter. "I'm your substitute cock?" It made sense now, the reluctance to take things to the next level and the distant look in his eye while we were fucking. He'd been someplace else, with someone else. Nausea rolled in my belly. "I could have been anyone? A fucking dildo?"

"Not anyone," Pieter said quietly. "It had to be someone I found attractive. Someone who wouldn't want more than just the sex."

*Me again?* If I waited for the steam to clear from between my ears, he may have had a point. "I was, what? Your mark?"

"You were available." Pieter moved into the hall. "That's what you were. And I'd rather not argue, so it's best you go." He gestured to the door. "Or do I have to call the police to have you removed?"

"Oh, don't worry. I'm only too happy to go." The sooner I got out, the sooner I could start forgetting this whole sordid afternoon had ever happened. I strode to the door, then paused.

"You know the saddest thing?" I turned around. Pieter stood halfway down the hall, nervously stepping from foot to foot. Tough tits if he didn't want to know, because I was going to tell him anyway. "I really fucking liked you."

He had the courtesy to flinch before I opened the front door and stormed away, determined never to think of him or his cartoon husband again.

# Chapter Nine

"Now, let's get this straight." Brian banged two pints of lager down onto the table. "Or is straight is the wrong word? Because if it was straight and you'd just rejected a hook up with a couple of nubile nineteen-year-old lesbians —"

"If they were lesbians, what would they need me for?" I grabbed the pint Brian had set down and took a long draft. I don't know why I was sitting here with him when I could be on the other side of the clubhouse working on getting myself laid by the brunette who'd been eyeing me up for days. But sex with a random wasn't on my mind and, if I was honest with myself, hadn't been for some time. "Don't you reckon I deserve the right to be the littlest bit gobsmacked that the guy I've been seeing the past couple of months is actually married?"

"Seeing?" The thick knot of Brian's eyebrow hitched up. "That's a first for you."

I slumped in my seat. "Yeah, well. I like him, don't I? Or thought I did."

"Prim little madam when you're in love, aren't you?"

"I'm not in love." I resisted the urge to swipe Brian upside his fat, balding head. "All he wants is a living, breathing sex doll as stand in for his frigid husband. Like I got no other value than my dick."

Brian studied me from over the top of his pint. "Not such a hot deal when the roles are reversed, is it?"

There were times when I could have done without Brian's words of wisdom, especially when I had nothing to counteract them with. "It's nothing like the same," I muttered, half-heartedly. "And I never said it wasn't a hot deal."

"Your thoughts followed a similar line to that blonde piece whose holiday you ruined the other week. What was her name?"

"Christ, you can be a knob sometimes." I downed most of my pint. I had no intention wasting any more drinking time pinned to this chair with Brian's lecturing doing my head in. "Want another?" I gestured to his mostly full glass.

"Can't, I'm driving. Told the missus I wouldn't be late. She knows the mate I've gone for a beer with is you."

"What's wrong with going for a beer with me?"

"No need to get narky. But it's not like your reputation doesn't precede you. She's worried you'll lead me astray. With the ladies."

*Lead him astray?* I couldn't be held responsible for his ogling every female guest under forty. In fact, my opportunities with the ladies dropped significantly whenever I showed up with Brian in tow. Which, for once, suited me. My head was full of Pieter and how Pieter wasn't who I'd imagined him to be in the part of my brain where I'd set us up together in the beginnings of a relationship.

"I'm not planning on leading anyone anywhere tonight. Except myself into a coma, with the aid of this." I waved my glass at him. "Any ladies, if you can find any in here, are safe as houses from me." I got up and staggered into the next table. It took a moment to get myself upright again, but I wasn't anywhere near drunk enough. The next table I bumped into would be the one I passed out on.

\* \* \* \*

I woke sometime the following day, face down on my bed, fully clothed minus shoes and my short-term memory. For the latter I was grateful, although my gratitude didn't extend as far back as the previous afternoon. My memory did. Pieter-with-an-i Croft had mugged me right off. Although it wasn't the first time in my life this had happened, it would damn well be the last.

I rolled over and dared to open my eyes. Light popped my retinas. I hugged a pillow to my face. How much had I drunk last night? Too many memories to drown, old and new. It was now the real suffering began.

I stumbled into the ensuite and ferreted my cock from my jeans. After I'd emptied my bladder, I scrubbed the pub carpet from my tongue with my toothbrush. Only then did I glance in the mirror above the sink and wished I hadn't. Hangovers didn't sit well with my fresh looks. Something about the dark circles under my eyes and the lax, uncomprehending expression on my face. That, and the mother of all headaches.

I opened the bathroom door. Voices drifted down the hall. I didn't remember switching on the TV last night, but neither did I recall coming home.

I'd taken two steps when I saw him. Feet up on the sofa, watching my TV like he had every right to be there.

"What. The. Fuck?" Forgetting the murky sludge last night's alcohol had made of my brain, I lurched into the lounge. "How'd you get in here?"

Pieter's husband barely glanced at me before refocusing on the TV. "Your door was open." He reached into the packet of biscuits sitting on his lap. "I did knock. You didn't answer."

"What's the deal?" I didn't understand anything about this kid. Not yesterday when I met him, or now when he'd made himself more than at home on my sofa. "Where's Pieter?"

"Dentist. He has a checkup." Nix munched down on a chocolate digestive, fixated on some kids' Saturday morning TV show. "He doesn't know I'm here."

Pieter probably didn't even know he'd had left the flat. Going out by himself didn't appear to be the done thing. Yet here he was with a packet of biscuits he'd raided from my cupboard and wearing another costume straight out of a charity shop bargain bin bucket. Most of it from the teenage girls' section.

I focused on his yellow socks. *One with a hole in the toe.* "Where're your shoes?"

"Over there." He waved a half-eaten biscuit toward the door, where a pristine pair of grey suede trainers sat together on the mat. "I have manners. I didn't want to get your carpet dirty."

"Your manners don't extend to showing up uninvited and randomly letting yourself into people's homes, I take it?" I sat on the sofa, by his outstretched feet. "Remind me why you're here, again."

"Because of Piet. You need to have sex with him."

"Right now?"

"No. He's at the dentist. I'm sure it wouldn't be allowed."

I picked up the remote and switched off the TV. This moment was so surreal I had to wonder if I wasn't still dreaming. *Nah.* If I had been dreaming, Pieter would be here instead of Nix. Naked.

"I don't get involved with married couples."

"Why not? Have you had previous experience?"

*What is this, a job interview?* I didn't have to tell him anything, but if it meant him leaving any quicker, I could offer a morsel or two. "I've been there and nothing worked out for me." In fact, it had worked itself into the worst few months of my life. Not something I'd voluntarily repeat.

"Did you have sex with both of them?"

"No. Just the wife." I don't know why I was telling a virtual stranger the details of my darkest days. But they weren't detailed details. Just the basics. He wasn't getting any more. "The husband knew nothing about it."

"Then what you had was an affair." His heavy tone left me in no doubt as to his opinion on affairs. "It wouldn't be the same with Piet."

"It sounds similar to me."

"Well, it isn't." Nix sat back in his seat. "Piet says you're good at sex. And he should know — he's had quite a few to compare you to."

And there was another choice snippet I could have done without hearing. The kid had just announced his husband was a slut. "Didn't he tell you I was too submissive?"

"He also said you give very thorough orgasms. And that's what most important about sex in the end."

I stared at him, at his expressionless face and the delicate sprinkle of biscuit crumbs dotting his lips. When the tip of his tongue peeked out to lick those crumbs away and a slow, totally inappropriate shiver danced up my spine, I forced myself out of my seat.

"I, uh, think I'll put the kettle on." I got up and made my way to the kitchen, unable to recall where the urge to throw him out had gone to.

"Green tea. No sugar," he called. "I'm sweet enough."

The TV went on as soon as my back was turned.

I didn't have green tea. I had regular tea in a bag, and he'd have to put up with it. I made myself coffee and spent more time than necessary in the kitchen so I could gather some wits about me.

I set two mugs on the coffee table. "How did you get here?" I asked, because as far as I knew, he could hardly walk anywhere and I didn't see any signs of the stick he'd had at his flat.

"Taxi. The driver brought me right to your door."

"How did you know which van was mine?"

"A fat, bald man in overalls told me. I think he works here."

*Fat. Bald. Overalls.* A near perfect description of Brian. *I bet he delighted in telling the kid where I lived.* He'd have already worked out who the violet-haired twink must be. "It's a good job I was in, wasn't it?"

"Your door was unlocked. Aren't you concerned about burglars?"

"I haven't got much to steal."

I didn't go in for decorative touches. Since I ate out most of the time, the place usually resembled an empty van awaiting guests. Possessions didn't interest me. My TV was a basic flat screen, not worth more than a couple of hundred quid. I had a laptop, but again, it was little more than basic spec. The most expensive item in here was my coffee machine. A Christmas present from my sister on a year where my folks hadn't bothered beyond a cash handout.

"I would have waited."

"Huh?"

"If you were out. I would have waited."

"I might've been gone all day."

"But you weren't. You were in bed, snoring. Very loudly."

I think I preferred it when he found the screen more captivating than me. "I don't see you getting home before Pieter at this rate. What'll he do when he finds out you're missing?"

"I'm not missing. I'm here with you." He pulled an aged mobile phone from the depths of his faded pink hoodie. "I have to keep this with me. Piet panics if I don't answer."

"What if he calls? Are you going to tell him you're with me?"

He gestured to the mug. "That isn't green tea."

"I'm all out."

"But I have green tea at home."

I stared at him, not for the first time wondering if he was a touch mentally challenged. "You're not at home, though, are you?"

His lips tightened. He pushed out a hand and left it poised mid-air. "I suppose it'll have to do."

Lazy little shit assumed I'd just hand the mug to him. I wasn't that subservient, despite what Pieter may have told him.

I picked up my coffee and took a sip. "What do you want? Aside from pimping out your husband."

"My tea?"

Fine. He could win this one. I handed him his sodding tea. "What else?"

He brought the mug very carefully to his lips, then pulled an unnecessary face. "It tastes bad." He handed the cup back. "You should come stay with us."

"Excuse me?" I almost dropped the damn cup before I could return it to the table. The kid was odd. Now I could add delusional to the list. Or he really was on the wind-up. A very professional wind-up. I wasn't even sure which applied to him.

"Just for one night. To begin with."

"Why, so you can teach me how to make green tea?"

"No. Piet makes good tea. You'd be there to have sex. We have already had this conversation."

Nix and Pieter might have had this conversation, but they hadn't let me in on their plans. "In case you hadn't noticed, I'm not so popular with your husband anymore."

"I know. You'd need to get popular again. Obviously."

Obviously. "How would I go about doing that?"

"Sex makes him happy."

As if it was that simple. He didn't seem to consider the very real possibility that Pieter would kick me out before I set foot over the threshold. I wasn't sure I had the energy to query his plan. One thing I did know — it was way past time for a smoke.

"You can't smoke around me," he said when I came back from the bedroom with a cigarette between my lips. "Nicotine makes me physically sick."

I set my lighter flame to the tip. "My house. My rules." I breathed a line of smoke at him. "You know where the door is."

Nix swung his feet off the sofa. "I need my shoes."

I hadn't expected that he'd take the leave option so easily. If I had, I would've have lit one up a lot sooner. "You know where they are, too."

"I'm taking these." He snatched the biscuits and got to his feet. "You're an awful host."

*An unwilling host, would be more accurate.*

Nix slipped one yellow-socked foot very carefully across the carpet. The little shit was playing me. He'd got here by himself. He'd walked up the steps, let himself in and snooped on me snoring in my bed. He could get his own shoes and he could show himself out the door. And call himself a taxi, because my brain was still too light in my skull to drive him anywhere.

# Chapter Ten

I didn't see him fall. I was too busy trying to ignore him. But a hard clunk and a sudden cry pulled me back to the moment.

He was on the floor in the kitchen, slumped against the front door, chocolate digestives scattered around him.

*What now?* I stubbed my cigarette out in the ashtray on the dining table. I had my doubts about his sudden fall being accidental, but I couldn't be sure.

"You okay?" I couldn't see his face, due to his hair hanging down like a gauzy curtain.

His chest hitched. "Go away."

"Bit difficult, seeing as this is my home."

"I'll need my shoes."

"You can't put them on yourself?"

He shoved his yellow-socked foot at me. "No."

I sank to my knees and picked up a shoe. "You are one weird kid, you know that?"

"I'm not a kid. And I'm ill." His scowl pushed into me as I levered his foot into his shoe. "There are things I can't do for myself."

There were a good few things he could do but chose not to. Such as working on his sex life with Pieter. "Have you ever wondered what might happen if you gave Pieter what he wants, so he doesn't have to go looking elsewhere?"

Phoenix lowered his gaze. "I bought some pills once. From the internet. But Piet wouldn't let me take them. He threw them down the toilet."

"Pills? Like, what, Viagra?" Just when I thought the kid couldn't come up with any more shocks for one morning.

He shook his head. "That's not what they were called."

*No, but that's what they basically were.* "Why would you want them in the first place?"

"Because there's something wrong with me. I thought they could fix me, but Piet said they wouldn't. He said they'd just make me—" A buzz vibrated the air. "That'll be Piet now."

"You going to answer?" I sat back on my heels. "You don't have to tell him you're here."

He brought the phone from his pocket. "Hello. No. I'm not at the library. I'm in Dean's caravan."

"Thanks, kid," I muttered. His visit was supposed to be secret. From everyone including me 'til he turned up. Pieter was going to be so pissed off, and not with his husband.

"I can call a taxi," Nix continued like he'd said absolutely nothing inflammatory so far. "No. He's been nice. Mostly. He wasn't so nice when he was smoking in front of me. I fell over trying to get away, and I'm still on the floor now."

I got up and eyed my cigarettes on the table, wondering how far another one would take Nix from my van.

"If you have to. Yes. He won't. I'm sure. Bye."

"I won't what?" I asked him from the sofa, where I was fuming as thoroughly as any lit cigarette.

"Touch me." Nix looked up at me from under his lashes. "In any way."

"I won't touch you. Fuck! What does he think I am?" I rammed my hands through my hair. "Is he coming here?"

"Yes." He slipped his phone back in his pocket. "To pick me up."

"I thought you didn't want him to know your whereabouts?"

"I won't lie to him to ease your conscience."

Not so much my conscience. Pieter would blame me for Nix being here, even though I had played no part except leaving a door unlocked. Again.

"Look. I apologize for lighting up in my home in front of an uninvited guest. Does that win me a brownie point or two?"

Nix stared at me with all that intense heat he had about him. "Don't you want to have sex with him again?"

We were right back more or less where we started. I lowered myself to the floor in front of him. Tying his laces was mostly a delaying tactic while I thought up a suitable reply.

"If it was just about sex, there wouldn't be a problem. But, and despite what your husband may think, I do have feelings. And I can't afford to waste any if I'm going to get nothing back."

"Why would you want to have feelings for Piet? You'd only be having sex."

That was it right there. I'd started having feelings. But I couldn't confess that to Pieter's husband. I barely even dared acknowledge that fact to myself. "Because sometimes these things happen. Unexpected things that no one can plan for. Not that it matters. Piet has made clear whatever plan you had for me is off." I finished tying his laces, then got up and offered out my hand.

Nix stared at my palm before taking it.

I pulled with enough force to get him on his feet. He staggered against me, trembling. Whether it was the result of his fall or of being so close to me, I didn't know.

I waited for him to rouse himself, yet he made no effort to move. This wasn't even a hug, when our arms hung by our sides. I don't know what it was, and I couldn't see his face to read what he thought. Not that his face ever gave much away.

If I stepped back, he'd fall over. I didn't know if that was worse than Pieter showing up to the sight of me and his husband sharing a moment in my van. In the end, I took Nix by his upper arms and gently guided him to the sofa.

That was where Pieter found us when he burst through the door some moments later, wielding a walking stick as though he fully expected to catch me mid-rape on his husband.

Nix and I couldn't have been farther apart and still be in the same room. I was by the TV, Nix by the door.

Pieter barely looked at me. He went straight to his husband and sank to his knees at Nix's feet. "Are you okay?"

"Perfectly well." Nix stared at Pieter's hand gripping his. "Why are you overreacting?"

I couldn't have asked better myself.

"I was worried. I always am when you head out alone without telling me." The walking stick thudded to the carpet. Pieter stroked his free hand through Nix's wispy hair. "Why here?"

An unspoken 'of all places' clogged the air.

"Someone had to." Nix yanked his hand free. "You said you'd rather cut off your testicles and pickle them for Christmas than breathe the same air as Dean again."

"Phoenix," Pieter hissed. "Can we go home and pretend this never happened?"

"He's been in a bad mood for days." Nix turned to me. "It's what happens when he doesn't get sex."

"For god's sakes, Phoenix." Pieter surged to his feet. "We're leaving." He snatched up the stick. "Are you going to walk, or do I have to carry you out?"

*Definitely carry.* The image of Pieter cradling Nix in his arms as they left my van together conjured up an intriguing scenario of the wicked things they might do to each other once they got home. Only there wasn't any possibility of them doing any wickedness together. If they did, neither of them would have any use for me.

"Why is he looking at us like that?"

I homed in on the moment. They were both staring at me, the subject of Nix's question. I hadn't realized I'd been staring at them in any particular way. But now my attention had been brought to it, I could see the disapproval in Pieter's face. Just as he could read the arousal in mine.

"He's drunk," Pieter said, with obvious disgust.

I glanced at my watch. "It's eleven thirty in the morning. Why the hell would I be drunk?"

"Then why don't you explain that look? In your own words." Pieter took a seat next to the immovable Nix and gestured that I should begin.

Seeing as I didn't have a death wish at that moment, I made something up. "I'm just tired, and I spaced out. Will that do you?"

"He doesn't look tired." Nix leaned closer to Piet. "He looks like he was thinking about sex."

Someone was constantly thinking sex, and it was the one person who claimed he didn't enjoy it. "Bedroom's end of the hall if you want to put your suspicions to the test."

Pieter sprang to his feet. He half-pulled, half-hauled Nix upright. "We need to leave now."

"I wouldn't mind if you want to go into Dean's bedroom," Nix said, taking hold of his stick. "I can wait in the car."

Pieter opened the van door. "I'm not having sex with Dean," he said, ushering Nix down the steps.

"You liked it enough the first time," I called after him.

Rather than continue to walk away from me as I had expected, he stamped back up the steps and into my van. "The first time would have been the last if I'd known then what a selfish, inconsiderate arsehole you are."

He wasn't telling me anything I didn't already know. "Just admit you couldn't keep away."

His nostrils flared. He looked so hot when he was about to blow a gasket. Even hotter, I imagined when he was about to blow me. But there was a fantasy best saved for another time.

"I came here for Nix. It had nothing to do with seeing you again."

"No?" I lit up a cigarette. Despite my heart skipping in my chest at the thought of a heated exchange, I remained calm in my seat. "You could have waited outside. No need to come in." I blew out a thin stream of smoke. "And judging by the speed you shot back in here, you couldn't wait, could you?"

Pieter's hand tightened on the door handle. "He said you left him on the floor."

"Better the floor than my bed." *Yeah, I shouldn't have said that.* But I'd done nothing here. We hadn't even been caught fucking, so I still didn't know what his actual problem was.

"Better anywhere than your bed."

"You weren't saying that a week ago." I stubbed out my cigarette in the ashtray. Beyond the window, I glimpsed a violet head disappearing into Pieter's little hatchback. "Phoenix invited me to come stay a night with you guys. Did you know that?"

"What?" Pieter drew the door closed. "You can't take that offer seriously."

*Wrong.* As far as I was concerned, it had been an invitation made in good faith, and if I had to use it to get under Pieter's skin, so be it. I'd just stomped my way into a minefield, but I couldn't bring myself to tiptoe back to safer ground. "He also said he'd wait in the car if you and me wanted to have a bit of a go-round in the bedroom. What'd you reckon?"

Pieter's eyes darkened. "You can have a bit of a go-round all right. In hell."

As he turned to leave, I grabbed his arm, harder than I'd meant to. I misjudged his size and his level of shock, which had taken all the weight out of him. He lost his footing and ended up flat on his back along the sofa where Nix had been sat so patient and silent for once while waiting for his husband to arrive.

Pieter punched his hips up, trying to dislodge me. "Let me go."

"In a bit."

"Let. Me. *Go*," he said, more forcefully, though his muscles were still slack even as my cock swelled against his hip.

"Not until after we've talked. Nix seems desperate to keep you happy, and he seems to think I can do that."

"My happiness is a long way from you."

I adjusted my weight and slid one hand between our bodies to the growing bulge behind his own fly. "Really?"

Piet fixed his focus on the dining table. "I can get sex anywhere."

"Now that sounds like something I'd say."

I must've hit a nerve, because his attention locked back on me. "I'm nothing like you. I don't con people into thinking they're in a relationship with me then dump them at the end of the week when something better comes long."

"I thought that was what you were into. No-strings sex." The fun of the situation fizzled as a possibility dawned on me. "Did you walk out on me because we were caught? Or because I asked you for a drink?"

"Going for a drink with you wouldn't have changed anything. It was just about the sex." He squirmed beneath me. "If you don't let go, I'll call the police and tell them you assaulted me."

"You'd have to get to your phone first. And tell your dick about the assault, because it's saying something different." I gave his cock another generous squeeze. "I'll need some time to think about this setup of yours."

"What?"

I slipped my legs to either side of him and sat up on his thighs. "You heard."

"I didn't make any offer."

"Your husband did on your behalf. He said you're not too pleasant to live with when you're not getting your regular dosage of dick."

"Phoenix did not say that."

"I'm paraphrasing. Are you saying it isn't true?"

"No. I do like to fuck. To be fucked. What of it?"

I couldn't believe I'd cast him as the uptight closet case. *It was a bit of a relief finding out that was exactly what he wasn't.*

"I feel the same. Only, lately, the only person I've wanted to fuck is you."

"Really?" He paused. "Why?"

"That's the thing." I dipped over him, close enough his breath wafted over my lips. "I've got no idea."

"Not my problem," he said, though some of the hostility had bled from his tone.

"It's our problem, I reckon."

"Why would you think so?"

"Because you and Nix have had actual conversations about where I'd fit into your lives. You ever do that about anyone else?"

"No, but—"

"Would you rather go back to getting your fill with randoms who might not be so accommodating when it comes to this whole 'no touching, no kissing' kink of yours?"

"It's not a kink. Phoenix is my husband. My kisses are for him."

"What about your touch?"

He looked away.

"Phoenix doesn't want your touch," I said, more to myself than to him. "But I do."

"Can you get off me now, please?" He still wouldn't meet my gaze. What was wrong with that violet-haired little gobshite? I'd have given half my family's fortune for one night of real, raw, no-holds-barred passion with this lad.

If I leaned over him any longer, I'd take something that wasn't mine. Like the kiss I'd craved since I'd met him. And since that would be a risk too far, I climbed off him. "Nix must be crazy not to want you."

Pieter wasted no time in scrambling off the sofa. "I wouldn't expect you to understand."

"I might if you explained it to me."

"What's the point? We won't be seeing each other again."

The air of finality in the last sentence was something I didn't want to hear. "Hey."

Piet stopped in the doorway. "What?"

"Can you give me a few days to think?"

"There's no need. Anything Phoenix said to you doesn't count. If he shows up again, which he won't, don't open the door."

"I didn't open the door. He let himself in."

Pieter hit the ground walking. "Then keep your door locked like everyone else."

"Pieter. Wait!" I jumped out after him, but he didn't look back. The car revved fast enough that the back wheel churned up grass in the push to get away.

"You got it bad." Brian stepped around the side of the van next to mine, a strange smile creasing his face.

"Got what bad?"

"Whatever it is with your gay swingers."

"They're not swingers." I was wasting my breath. How could I tell him I suspected one-half of their partnership was as near as damn it a virgin? "Were you spying on me?"

"Nope. Was just changing a bulb in there." He gestured to the van he'd been hiding behind. The van he probably hadn't set a foot inside. "You should thank me. I could've told that lad I'd never heard of you."

"I wish you had," I said, knowing that wasn't quite true. Pieter's visit had given me a lot to think about. If having Pieter in my bed meant I'd have to share him with Nix, that was something I could learn to live with. *Rather than not having him at all?*

Brian moved closer. "What were you three doing in there together?"

"Not what you imagine we were doing."

"I'm imagining nothing." Brian raised both hands. "Strictly a heterosexual thinker, me. But I bet they'd tear in half real easily. There's nothing to either of them."

"Does everything have to be about sex with you?" I asked as I made my way to my van.

"No, but isn't that what they want you for?" Brian asked, trailing along behind me.

*In a word, yes.* Right there was the raw truth. If I could live with that, the three of us would get along fine.

"You reckon I'd be crazy to turn them down then, yeah?" I asked as Brian followed me inside.

"Like I said, if they were a couple of hot lezzies—"

I waved my hand to indicate there was no need for him to continue.

Ash Penn

"But now you know the score, what's to stop you? It's not like there's going to be any emotional connection going on."

I stopped what I was doing. Mainly, reaching for the kettle to make Brian a brew. "You don't think blokes can fall in love with each other?"

"That's not what I said. I thought you gave up on romance after that business with Trudy. Once bitten and all that."

I barely even winced at mention of her name anymore. That was progress. Still, emotions had a habit of creeping up on me when I wasn't looking. With Trudy, I'd lumbered straight in. Now here I was, doing it again. As if no lesson had ever been learned. Still, Brian was right about one thing. There was no possibility of acting as an unwitting sperm donor for Pieter. "You want tea, right?"

"And a smoke if you got one going spare." Brian took a pew on my sofa in his work-stained overalls. "You planning on giving the pair of them the boot before you've even given them your dick?" He lifted one of his mud-caked steel-toecaps in a kicking motion before returning the grimy sole to the carpet. I had underestimated how important Nix's manners were.

"I don't know. I'm thinking over my options." If this was only about the sex, there would be no issue. I'd started feeling something for Pieter, feelings that would get complicated further along the line. But if it came down to a choice between getting too involved and not getting involved, I knew which way I was going to fall. Because the truth was, I'd half-fallen his way already.

# Chapter Eleven

I wrestled with my head, heart and options for another couple of days or so. No, that wasn't quite true. I'd made up my mind the day Pieter had stormed out of my van demanding that I leave him alone, but it had taken me two days to finally approach his flat and give him the good news.

It was eight-thirty in the evening. I'd come straight from a shower after work, armed with an overnight bag and a decent supply of condoms. Did I think I'd get to use them? No, but Pieter would know I was serious about giving this thing a go.

I rang the buzzer. Twice. They could have gone out. I didn't see Piet's car anywhere close to the building. But Nix was cultivating some serious prison pallor. I bet he rarely left the flat, aside from when he was making a nuisance of himself at other people's homes.

I waited until someone was coming out of the door, then slipped inside.

At their door, I knocked twice. Two firm raps. I was about to settle down for a long wait when the door clicked open.

Nix stood there, hair pale and tangled, dressed in a pair of giant's pajamas. "Piet said if you stopped by, I wasn't to open the door."

"But here you are."

"You might have the stamina to knock all night, but I don't have the energy to listen to it." He drew back the door. "I'm not inviting you in, but I can't stop you if you insist. Are you insisting?"

I nodded.

"Then I have no choice."

I stepped through the door. Nix's gaze dropped to my bag. "Have you left home?"

"Nope. Just taking up your offer to stay. If Pieter will agree."

"I invited you. So he has to. Bedroom's in there." He waved toward a door on his left.

"Cheers." I might get to stay 'til morning if I could persuade Nix to leave off notifying Pieter of my presence. I opened the door. The light was on. Beneath the bare bulb sat a double bed, unmade. A chest of drawers littered with hair care paraphernalia, Nix's at a guess. "Isn't this your room?"

"Yes. You can have sex in here. I'll be asleep when you do it, so I won't hear or see anything if you're shy."

*Shy?* I assumed he was joking, but there wasn't a spasm of humor anywhere on him. "I'll take the sofa." I studied his face, looking for any hint that this whole thing had been about winding me up. "If it's all the same with you."

"It makes no difference to me where you have sex. There's blankets in there." He pointed to a black ottoman at the foot of the bed. "The sofa turns into a bed. I'll help you with it."

*I'd rather help myself to a separate bed than to Pieter under Nix's watchful gaze.*

I left my bag in the hall while I went to fetch the blankets. "Do you often have guests to stay?"

"Piet's other men? No."

*Other men? How many have there been? Or are still around now?* Nix wasn't the right person to ask, even if it had been any of my business. I took out a sheet and a blanket from the box. "So this is new to all of us."

"Yes." Nix picked up my bag and shuffled down the hall. "Although it was all my idea."

I was still painfully aware of whose idea this was. And Piet's thoughts on the matter. Still, there was always room to get him to change his mind and come around to Nix's way of thinking. I set the lid back on the ottoman, and armed with my bedding I followed Nix into the lounge.

It was cooler in there than the last time. The light was on, but the fire was off. The central heating was still pumping out a fair bit of hot air.

"Piet needs sex." Nix grabbed the sofa cushions and set them on the floor. "You are the perfect solution."

I set down the blankets and pulled out the bed base. "Might've been more perfect if I'd have known the situation from the start."

"He never found the right time to ask. But he does want this to happen."

"You think?" I didn't believe Pieter liked me in the same way I liked him, in the way I couldn't explain. "He wasn't too welcoming the other day."

"That's because he doesn't want to admit he wants you." Nix handed me the sheet. "You'll have to make the rest up yourself. I'm too exhausted to help."

He didn't look anywhere near as exhausted as he had earlier, but I made up the bed without complaint and even kept my mouth shut when Nix climbed in and snuggled under the blanket.

"If you want tea," he said, as if us sharing a bed was going to be perfectly natural, "you'll have to make it yourself. There's macaroni cheese in the fridge, too, if you're hungry. Piet made it. With bacon." He grabbed a remote, and the TV flickered to life.

"I'm not hungry." I brought out my cigarettes, then caught the horror in Nix's face. I couldn't smoke around him. I especially couldn't smoke around him in his own home. "Sorry." I set the pack back in my pocket. "You, ah, planning on sticking around?"

"Yes. I live here." He settled back against the cushions and pointed to the TV cabinet. "There's a *Star Wars* DVD over there. Fetch it for me."

No 'please'? I could imagine this was life for Pieter, fetching and carrying after his diva. Still, if I was to survive the night, it was best I stayed in Nix's good books.

I retrieved his DVD, a boxset of the original three films. *The only three worth watching.* "You want me to put one on?"

"No, I want you to bring it to me."

*Bossy couple of twinks, these two. What would it be like, getting bitch-slapped between them daily?* If me and Pieter were to be longer-term, I'd get to find out quickly. I handed over the DVD. Pieter had a point about my submissiveness, although to my knowledge no one had made comment before.

Nix opened the case. He didn't take out a DVD. What he brought out were a couple of ready-rolled joints in a small see-through bag, which he held up between us. "Would you like to share?"

"Where did you get that?" I sounded disapproving, which I most definitely wasn't. I hadn't been expecting him to pull those out.

"Our usual supplier." Nix drew out one of the fatties. "Lighter."

As I gazed at his outstretched palm, my mind pictured him and Pieter in bed, naked and sweaty. Another fantasy session I couldn't bring myself to wish away. Wrapped in each other's arms, the air swimming with sex and the sweeter aroma of Mary Jane. I photoshopped myself lying between them, their warm bare legs, one each side of me, their soft, sated cocks resting against my hips.

Arousal tingled in my balls. I handed Nix the lighter before perching on the bed.

Nix struck a flame and set the tip to the twisted end of the joint. The paper flared, the weed within burning bright orange. He tipped his chin and exhaled. The loose folds of his pajama top sagged around his narrow chest. "Cinder brought this down to us from London last week. Do you like it?"

"Cinder? As in Rella?"

Nix cracked open an eye. "Cinder as in Keel. She used to be Winterson, but then she married Greg. He's a Keel." He offered out the joint. "She grows her own."

"Your dealer is a relative?"

"She's not a dealer. She's my mother. Are you going to take a hit on that or let it burn?"

*His mother?* Made sense. Cinder and Phoenix. *And I thought my folks were dysfunctional.* I joined him against the sofa cushions, then set the paper to my lips.

The smoke wisped through my lungs, glazing me in a gentle fog. It wasn't overpowering or mind-shifting. More like a generous hug I could quite easily bask in all night.

"Give it to me. My need is greater." Nix plucked the joint from my fingers all too soon. "Your problems aren't physical."

The weed eased the tension from my muscles and my brain. I chanced asking the question that had been bugging me since we'd met. "What have you got? I mean, your illness."

Nix squinted at me through a fog of sickly smoke. "CFS. Or ME. It's the same thing."

"ME? Like Stephen Hawking?" I couldn't imagine Nix, all twisted up and wasting in a wheelchair. The thought chilled me enough I quickly shoved that image to the back of my brain.

"No." Nix's pupils dilated. "That's motor neurone disease."

Relief threaded through my veins, as fuzzy satisfying as the weed. That illness I wouldn't wish on anyone. He sank into the cushions, his lashes barely visible. I could only see them because of the violet shadows beneath. The same shade as in his hair.

"You're thinking of MS. Everybody does." His lips parted in a generous yawn. His tongue sat pink and plump in the velvet depths. Another vision flashed into my mind, of my fat engorged cock deep into the soft, wet tunnel of his throat.

I was now coveting a raging hard-on while discussing his health. *Classy.* "Is there a cure?"

"No. Some people don't believe it's a genuine illness."

I could tell whatever he had was a real thing by looking at him. "What does it do? I know you have trouble walking and with your muscles, but is it more than that?"

"Yes. A lot more. But can the questions wait until Piet gets home? I don't want to talk about it now."

I stole another toke. "Yeah, if you like." I doubted I'd have the opportunity to question him about anything once Pieter got home.

"Good. Don't breathe out." Before I could raise my eyebrows, Nix climbed into my lap. He was light as a breeze. No adult male should feel so fragile, so insubstantial. Pieter was practically a body-builder by comparison.

Nix leaned close, his mouth slightly open. I realized what he had in mind a split second before his lips touched mine. They were as cool as his fingertips, but this wasn't a kiss. I wouldn't have accepted an actual kiss.

When his fingers clamped down on my shoulders, I released the tug of smoke. He inhaled, sucking in the second-hand hit. As he breathed out, his muscles softened. His eyelids drooped in what I took for pleasure. "Hmm. Now that could almost pass for erotic."

# Chapter Twelve

Spending time in bed with Pieter's husband didn't unnerve me as much as I thought it might. Not since I'd loaded myself up with the Dutch courage. I was comfortable enough, chilling with him and making out like nothing else existed beyond these walls.

"I'm having a good day today," Nix said, pushing a palm to my slowly rousing cock.

"Because I'm here?" I was beginning to slur my words. The weed held me in a daze, while Nix sat astride me, pinning me to the mattress. *A dangerous game, this.* But all the best games were.

"No. A good day because I've spent half of it awake." Nix squeezed me through the denim. "I've never touched another man's penis before. Only Piet's."

"Do you want to touch another man's penis?" I asked. Or prompted. I wasn't quite sure which.

"I don't know. I'm curious."

"Not...horny?" My solid, pulsing bulge under his fist betrayed how I felt about this situation, but Nix remained coolly impersonal.

"No." He let go of my shaft and stole the joint from my fingers. "I don't get sexually aroused."

"What, at all?" Everyone got horny, didn't they? Some more than others, but still. If I was married to Pieter, I'd be nailing him twenty-four-seven.

"I don't like sex." Nix chugged on the joint before passing it back. "What changed your mind?"

"Nothing. I've always liked sex."

He looked at me like I was an alien. "About staying here. For one night. With Piet."

"Oh." I shifted my free hand to his hip. "You did." The prominent bone fit neatly in my palm. "When you came to see me. I was pissed off, before. I just needed time to come to terms." The pressure of his palm sent a hot, spiraling fire the length of my cock. "You sure he's going to be okay about this?"

"About what?"

"Me and you. In this bed. Together." I guessed he must be, since Nix seemed more than willing to share Piet with me. Or was that the weed and my testosterone reasoning my sanity away?

"I don't need permission." Nix dropped the joint into the ashtray on the arm of the sofa. "Piet does what he wants. I can do the same." He shuffled closer. His arse pressed against my dick. "I'm a bonus."

"That a request?"

"What do you mean?"

"Bone us. That's what you said." I laughed, although to be fair it was more of a giggle. Damn weed had gone straight to my head.

Nix sat above me, rigid as my cock, exquisite yet somehow vacant. "Why are you laughing?"

"Never mind. It's just that he didn't tell me about you. Not a clue. Not even a wedding ring." I unclamped my hand from his hip and touched the silver band on his finger. "This is nice."

"Yes." He pulled his hand away. "Piet doesn't wear his to work."

I slipped my arm around his tiny waist. His frailty distracted me for a second. What this kid needed was a few hearty meals inside him. Someday soon I'd take them both to dinner, if Pieter could bear to sit at the same table with me. Afterward, I'd show the pair of them what submissive wasn't.

Nix slipped his palms down my chest and pushed his fingertips under the hem of my jumper. "How am I doing?"

"How are you doing what?" I asked carefully, in case it was a trick question. Although Nix didn't do trick, or jokes. He was on the level. All the time.

"Seducing you, of course. I've never done it before."

"You must've seduced Pieter at some point."

"Piet doesn't count."

Did Piet know he didn't count? I shifted under his chilled touch. "You just said you weren't into sex."

"This isn't sex. It's exploring." He tugged at my jumper. "Take this off."

To do so, I'd have to start with my jacket. I shrugged out of that, then my jumper. Half-naked, I brushed my fingers under his voluminous pajama top. "Now you show me some skin."

"No." He yanked his top down. "You don't want to see."

"Who says I don't?" I went to reach for him, gently teasing. Nix clung to his clothing like I might literally tear it from his now trembling body. "Sorry," I said, letting him go. He was as extreme as Pieter when presented with a blowjob offer.

"My body's not like yours." Nix reached for the half-smoked joint. He took a toke, keeping his head lowered. His fringe hung down into his eyes, violet strands as fine as his cheekbones.

"You think you're the best judge of whether someone else finds you attractive?" I took a chance and rested my hands on his thigh. "I wouldn't have you down for the shy type." His husband had wasted no time in getting naked. There wasn't a gram of self-consciousness with that guy.

"I'm not." He held out the joint, which I readily accepted. "This is just a game."

"You know he wouldn't let me kiss him when we were fucking?"

Nix's hazy eyes widened. "Why not?"

"Maybe he thought it'd count as being unfaithful to you." I sucked in a drag, enough to coat my lungs in a thick, honeyed smog.

"I like to kiss," Nix said simply. "I like kissing you."

I liked kissing him, too. A worthy substitute, since Piet was so precious about his own lips. "You want another?"

When Nix gave an enthusiastic nod, I yanked him forward. Our mouths bumped together. I breathed out, feeding the smoke from my lungs to his.

Nix's fingers migrated to my fly. He tugged at the button, then pulled at the zip. I held the kiss, flicked my tongue into his mouth as his cold touch closed around my naked shaft.

"Huffffh." Nix groaned into my mouth.

I skipped my fingers to his cheeks and broke the kiss. "What?"

"Your penis." His grip cinched tighter. "It's bigger than Piet's. Way bigger."

Not what I'd been expecting, but I wasn't going to argue. "Is that an issue or a compliment?"

"It's a statement of fact. We're not going to have sex. I'm just exploring."

I stifled the urge to laugh. Not at him, although he'd take it as such. Both him and his husband could entertain me in bed and out of it. "I don't think Pieter would want us to, anyway.

Nix tensed again. "I don't need his permission. I'm not a part of him. I'm independent."

"I know that." I pressed another kiss to his lips. I didn't want to kick off an argument about skewed morals. I didn't even disagree with what he'd said. "But you made it clear to me you weren't a part of the arrangement."

"I can explore, though." Nix slid his fist up my shaft. His thumb slid back my foreskin. A sweet fire crackled down my spine. Whatever he may or may not have done before, he'd learned how to handle a cock.

"And what do you want to do, while you're exploring?" I sank into the cushions, the line I'd drawn not so clear to me anymore. "Your call."

Disappointingly, he unfurled his fist from my shaft. "Can we kiss some more?"

"Much as you like." *Weird kid.* But his kisses were welcome.

Nix plucked the joint from my fingers and pushed it into the ashtray. He leaned close, and touched his lips to mine. The TV played in the background, melting the air further. The kiss warmed me because it was slow, languid, like it meant more than it did.

Nix tilted his head. His hair veiled one eye. Considering he said he knew very little about seduction, he looked sexy as fuck. "Piet never kisses me like that."

"Why not?" Seemed he craved my kisses. Why wouldn't Piet want to do the same?

"He sees my illness first and me second."

"Have you told him that?"

"Yes, but he doesn't listen." Nix climbed off me, leaving my dick hard and wanting something I clearly wasn't going to get. He picked up the remote control and switched off the TV. The room dissolved into blackness. "If he sees you, he'll throw you out. I'll stay. Then I can explain why you're here."

"Thanks," I muttered.

My body was still smoldering in frustration, and in almost no time, Nix was snoring gently beside me. As tempted as I was to slip one off under the covers, I resisted. My only hope was that Pieter might like to play firefighter when he got home.

# Chapter Thirteen

I woke to a loud screech and a vise-like grip pinching my arm. I opened my eyes. A light blazed directly above my head. The harsh noise blasted my ear again. This time I could make some sense out of the sound.

"Get out! Out of this bed. Out of my flat!"

"Our flat," a more reasoned voice said beside me.

The grip on my arm yanked harder. I went with it, sitting up and waiting for my head to clear. I squinted at the face in front of me. A very red-cheeked irate face. "Piet?"

"It's Pieter," he said through gritted teeth. "I want you out."

"I got that impression."

"Have you touched him?" Pieter stepped back. No, he more fell at the thought of his precious husband getting treated to a portion of what he himself had enjoyed not so long ago.

"We haven't had sex."

I switched my attention to Nix. He sat beside me, hair like a frayed tapestry. His voice was solid, though. Deadly calm.

"He's right," I said. "We haven't."

Pieter's eyes glinted with undiluted malice. "Get dressed and get out. Or I call the police."

"The police?" I couldn't help myself. I laughed. Too hard. This was the third time he'd threatened me with the law and it was no less amusing than the first. "What are they going to charge me with? Sliding skin with your more-than-up-for-it husband?" As soon as the words were out, I regretted them. A slight despairing tremor tugged at Pieter's lower lip. A tremor that hit me low in the belly. I swallowed. "Nothing happened," I said quietly. "We only shared a smoke and the mattress." And a bit of spit when we kissed. I wouldn't mention that, though.

"Piet?" Nix pried himself from the bed. "We need to go to our room." He edged closer to his husband, stiff-legged and hunched over. Earlier, he'd been the most animated I'd seen him. Now his voice sounded raw and slurred with interrupted sleep.

"I want him out. He's not welcome here."

"He is. I invited him. I can do that. It's my home, too."

Pieter opened his mouth, but instead of speaking he flashed his killer glare. "First thing in the morning, I want him gone." He spun around and stormed from the room.

I wasn't sure what to do next, so I waited. In bed, covers back. I had my jeans on. I'd even managed to sneakily fasten my fly.

Rather than go after Piet, Nix remained in the doorway, hovering. "You can't leave," he said, like I'd made any move to do so. Which I hadn't. Yet.

"Why can't I?"

"Because you've smoked too much to drive."

"Thanks, officer, I'll bear that in mind." I could still drive. Or call a cab. It was only my ego that had thought I could spend the night here, and my stubbornness held me in that bed as firmly as any embrace. "I'm not going anywhere." To demonstrate, I sank back into the cushion.

"Where are your car keys?"

"In my jacket. Why?"

Nix edged back into the room and plucked my jacket off the floor. "You can have this back in the morning."

So he didn't trust me. *Nice.* Did he think I wasn't serious about giving their idea for me a go? We needed to discuss this if Piet could ever deign to speak to me again. "Can I get some sleep now?"

"Yes. Of course." He reached for the light. "Good night, Dean." The bulb above my head flickered out.

"Yeah," I muttered. "Nite."

After he'd gone, I lay listening to my own breaths in an effort to distract from the thoughts whizzing round my head. Somewhere along the line, I'd misunderstood what this arrangement was supposed to be. If Nix was willing to share Piet with other men, then I'd assumed the same would apply to Nix.

Piet had almost combusted at the merest possibility I'd touched his precious husband the other day in my van. That should have been clue enough to keep my testosterone to myself.

I knew Nix was off limits. I just hadn't wanted him to be. So what did that make me? Nothing new. This was what I spent my time doing. The only difference was I usually got rid of one before starting on the next. *Nix's kisses and that bloody stash of weed. A lethal combination.*

How Piet could believe his own husband wasn't into sex when he kissed like that, I didn't know.

I was still too fuzzy in my own head to fathom it out.

I only closed my eyes for a second. The next thing I knew, natural daylight was falling on my face. The curtains at the patio doors were now open to the courtyard garden.

Behind me, the sound of clattering dishes from the kitchen indicated I wasn't alone. I rolled over. The arm of the sofa prevented me from seeing who was in the kitchen, but I knew the answer. The angry battering was a passive-aggressive din that could be coming from only one person.

"Tea?" A face swam into view above. Mousy hair, sandy freckles, no glasses. *Trick question?* "I'm also doing bacon and eggs with toast and mushrooms. Interested?"

I rammed my brain into first gear. What was his game? I wasn't awake enough yet to figure it out, so I went along with the charade. "Yeah. I guess."

"Good." The stiff face forced a smile. "Won't be long."

I sat up. Pieter had his back to me, stirring eggs in a pan. The air thickened with the meaty aroma of bacon. His attitude unnerved me, not least of all because of the screaming banshee he'd been the night before.

I grabbed my jumper off the floor and put that on. I needed some thinking space. And that wasn't all. "Where's the bathroom?"

"Down the hall. Opposite the bedroom." He said this while he worked, like I was a real and welcome guest.

I found the bathroom, which was more of a shower room. Just a toilet, sink and a simple shower cubicle complete with hand rail and a seat that pulled down from the wall. A selection of toiletries was lined up on a shelf under the window. Fruity shower gels and expensive shampoos, the latter presumably Nix's. I fancied a shower to wash off last night's sweat, but I couldn't risk taking that liberty. Not when I was close to being thrown out on my ear.

When I returned to the kitchen, Piet was still busy at the hob.

I took a seat at the small table. There was a large plate of all the breakfast Pieter had promised steaming in front of me. "How's Nix?" I asked to break the silence.

"Asleep." Piet set a mug of tea down on the table. Strong, with only a touch of milk. "I haven't poisoned it. Or the food. Nix convinced me not to."

"You said he was asleep."

"He is. It was last night when he did the convincing."

I picked up my knife and fork. Food looked that good, I'd risk the poison. "What else did you decide?"

"That I overreacted."

And right there was understatement of the year. "Nothing happened," I reminded him. "All we did was talk. You and me have done more."

Piet spooned more egg onto a fresh plate, then came and took the chair opposite me. "We've never kissed."

Nix had told him about that, then. It was just as well he'd cried off before I'd encouraged him for more. Damn weed made him horny to the point of crazy. I'd have to have been totally mental to have thought Piet wouldn't mind what I got up to with his little cock-tease of a husband.

"That's your issue, not mine." I waited, a forkful of eggs poised an inch from my lips, half-expecting a whack with the still-hot pan. I'd have done the same in his position, if I had a significant other. Or was ever likely to get one. "Look." I lowered my fork. "Last night shouldn't have happened. Not that anything did. I just got the idea that you two weren't averse to…" How did I put this without causing him to kick off again? "Experimenting."

"Experimenting?" The air crackled. "Do you find him attractive?"

Now there was a loaded question. I shoveled the eggs into my mouth. They were good. Well-seasoned, with a pleasant tang of mature cheese. "Hmm." I reloaded my fork. "If I'd have known you could cook like this, I would've had you sent to my van first thing every morning."

"Because Phoenix thinks you're beautiful."

The second mouthful stuck in my throat mid-swallow. "What?" I spluttered, dislodging the last piece of egg. "He said that?"

Piet nodded. "Now he's formed his opinion, and nothing will change it."

"Not even you?"

"I've stopped trying. Which is why we need to talk. About what we're going to do. About…"

"Us fucking again?"

As quickly as he'd lifted himself up, he slumped in his chair. "Do you think we can do this without the ego trip?"

"The fucking? Or the —"

"The talk." Piet briefly closed his eyes. When he opened them, the whites looked even more brilliant due to the redness of his cheeks. "This was much easier to deal with when Nix and I were —"

"Fantasizing?"

Piet set down his knife and fork. They hadn't gone anywhere near his plate. "Will you please stop finishing my sentences."

Was I? Only to get to the part where he invited me into his bed. I hadn't decided whether his bed was where I wanted to be. "Am I finishing them all wrong?"

"No. But if we're having a conversation, I'd quite like to be a part of it."

Fair enough. I scooped more egg onto my fork. "Go ahead. I won't interrupt again."

"You were supposed to be a one-off. Like the others."

"How many others?" So much for not interrupting. But finally, the chance to ask. I pictured a conveyer belt of other blokes, used once then stuffed back on, never to be seen again. I don't know why that bothered me. Brian would tell me I did the same thing, only mostly with women. I did try with the girls while I was seeing them. It wasn't all about the sex.

"Six."

"I'm your seventh?"

"No. Five others. Then you. Six in total."

Six wasn't so many. Not when I did four plus in a month. *Sounds like a hell of a lot of sex over the course of the year. Definitely man-whorish.* Never had cause to think of it that way before.

"It's not cheating. Nix always knows." He sat back in his chair. "Now you're looking at me like I'm perverted as well as loose."

"Loose? Ha." Memories of his arse sent a thrill clean through me. "I don't think there's anyone who's going to accuse you of being loose."

"You know what I meant."

"I'm not disapproving. Who am I to tell you two how to live?"

"But?"

"I'm not the morality police. However…" I flashed a smile. "We're people, not robots. Can either of us guarantee this won't get complicated?"

Piet pushed his plate away. For the first time, I noticed he was wearing a ring, too. The same as Nix's. A plain silver band. A simple sign of ownership. "Why'd you think I never let you kiss me? It's not because I have some weird aversion to intimacy. I'm married to someone I love, but I need more than he can give me."

It made sense. I would have understood so much better had I known from the off. I wouldn't have let my mind wander toward a relationship, for one. "But you do have a sex life with Nix. Don't you?"

"Nix is ill a lot and he's never been interested in that side of our life together."

"I didn't get the impression he wasn't interested."

"In you?" Piet let out a bitter laugh. "Oh, you're different. He's definitely interested in you."

"And not you?"

"If he was, we wouldn't need you."

I knew what he was saying. And why they might want to spice things up with a third party. But Piet's reluctance sat there like a transparent wall between us. I wasn't sure how I'd take to being the expendable one.

"Nix thought it would be a good idea," Piet said, filling the silence I'd left. "I mean, about me and you. I told him you and I were compatible sexually. Then —"

"You told him I was good in bed." I couldn't resist a grin as I translated his words. "I mean, despite the whole submissive thing."

Piet winced. "I didn't say that exactly. I..." He sucked in a breath. "It doesn't matter what was said. Nix wanted me to tell you, and I was going to. But —"

"I didn't get that memo." If I had, what would I have done? I wouldn't have dismissed the idea so readily had I been pre-warned. Nix might be ill, but he carried a waiflike aura I wouldn't ordinarily go for, if I believed in auras. People who had mothers that went by the name of Cinder and grew their own weed, those were the folk who believed in auras. I bet Nix did, too. If he'd read mine, he'd seen something that attracted him to me as well.

"I wasn't actually planning on telling you about him. Or any of it." Piet collected a bird's portion of egg on his fork. "I wanted to keep us separate."

"Then why'd you tell your husband about me?"

"Because it's a rule. I always tell him if I get with someone."

"You told him about every time you and me...?"

His blush told me all I needed to know.

"Are you going to finish that?" I asked. Those eggs were too good for the bin.

"I'm not hungry." He rose from the table. He opened a cupboard above the worktop and drew out half a dozen bottles of pills.

"Is all that for Nix?"

"Yes. They're vitamins, mostly." He popped a few lids, then started doling them out into a compartmentalized pill box. "Not as scary as they look."

"Must be tough, though." Toughest job in the world. Caring for someone he loved, someone who was the same age, someone he was married to. The pair of them were alone and not even out of their teens.

"It could be worse." Piet grabbed a bottle of mineral water from the fridge, then slipped the pill box under his arm. "There's hope one day he might get well again." There was an unspoken addition to the sentence. *Get well and want to fuck*, although I wasn't so sure Nix being ill and his lack of a conventional sex drive were related.

Piet disappeared into the hall and returned a few minutes later. He reached into the oven, pulled out another plateful of breakfast and slapped it down in front of me. "Nix isn't hungry, so you can have this one as well."

Third helping. Well, two and a half. I piled all the food onto one plate, then made a start.

"Were you planning on stopping by again tonight?" That was way more accusation than question. "Only, I have work."

"No. I only stayed to see how long it would take for you to throw me out. I never took Nix's invitation seriously." I also hadn't expected to have shared a bed with him for part of the night, or everything else that had happened. Alcohol scattered my memory, but weed refined it. I recalled every kiss, every touch. And wanting more than Nix was prepared to give.

"We do need to talk, though. If this is going to happen."

"Agreed." I shoved the sexy times with Nix out of my head. There wasn't a chance of me talking about that again. This was about me and Piet. "When?"

"Give me your number. I'll call you."

"Will you, though?"

"If I say I will."

"It's just that usually the only call you want to make is to the cops."

"Since we're going to happen, there's no point fighting the inevitable."

We were inevitable now? I didn't know about that. Why should I? The pair of them told me virtually nothing about their own plans. I was expected to go along with whatever.

"When should I expect your call?"

"I don't know. Soon."

"Kind of vague for something that's inevitable."

*I said inevitable, didn't I? Not predictable.*

# Chapter Fourteen

"Dean?" Piet sounded uncertain. Had he assumed I'd given him the local Chinese takeaway number instead of mine? Still, my heart did an enthusiastic flip. It had been a few days since I'd last heard his voice.

"Hey."

"Are you busy?"

*Hello to you, too.* "I've just finished work." Strolling home beneath a still warm sun, ready for an evening in front of the TV with a pizza. Unless a better offer presented itself.

"Could you come round?"

"I don't know," I said, trying to keep every spark of enthusiasm inside my chest and out of my voice. Right there was the better offer. I had thought I might have to show up at the flat, armed with my overnight bag again. "I'll need to check my diary."

"Oh. If you've got plans —"

"I didn't say I had plans." I'd forgotten how highly strung he could be. I'd hoped he'd given up on the hostility, since he was the one making the call. "What time do you want me?"

He paused. "It's not for what you're thinking."

I slowed my pace. "What am I thinking?"

"I need you to sit with Nix. Can you do it?"

I stopped walking. He wanted me to sit with the same man he'd wanted me arrested for sitting with a few nights before? Was this progress? "Any particular reason?"

"He's has had a bad couple of days and I can't take another evening off work. I'm still on a trial and I'll get fired."

"I can come round." That wasn't the issue. "It's just, you trust me with him?"

"I want you to watch him, Dean. Not sleep with him."

There he was. The fiery side of Piet that got my dick hard and made my blood sizzle.

"Do I get to sleep with you?" I didn't think the request was unreasonable. This wasn't about me and Nix. This was about me and Piet. Although we had yet to define what 'this' was.

Silence blunted the line. Like the thought of spending the night with me was an actual chore. "Bring your overnight things. We'll see about anything else."

\* \* \* \*

He answered the door in his supermarket finery of black trousers and dark blue fleece, stressed round the eyes and haggard around the shoulders.

"You okay?" I asked as he let me in. Considering what had happed the first two times I'd shown up here, not getting shouted at and threatened with the police was a pleasant change.

"It's not me who's ill. Nix has been throwing up for most of the day."

That'd explain this whole exhausted look. "Who do you usually get to sit with him while you're working?"

"We have a neighbor. She's old, and she likes to take care of us. But she's on holiday and so it was you or no one."

"No one wasn't available, either?"

Piet's face instantly shut down. "You can leave if you're going to be like that."

*Message received.* I closed the door in case he had any ideas about chucking me out. "I'm happy to be here."

"Good." Piet gestured for me to follow him down the hall to where the sofa bed still dominated the lounge.

I perched on the mattress. "Should I take this as my official invitation to stay the night?"

"Nix has been using that bed for most of the day." He grabbed a comb and started fussing at his damp hair in the wall mirror. "I haven't had the chance to put it away."

I stood up a lot faster than I'd sat down. "Has he puked on it?"

Piet stopped short of rolling his eyes. "No. He hasn't puked on it."

"In that case…" I kicked off my shoes and swung my legs up on the sofa. "How about you come and spend a touch of quality time with me before you head off?"

Piet set his comb down on the coffee table. "I don't have time for quality anything. I need to go. Have I told you about the bell?"

"Huh?"

He gestured to the bookcase. "The receiver is there on the shelf. When Nix rings, it means he needs something. He probably won't. He told me not to call you. Not until he was well again. But I was desperate."

I tried not to let my disappointment show. "Makes me feel right special, that."

"I didn't mean—"

"I know." I grinned. Piet tended to understand humor only slightly more than Nix did. "I've been responsible for you leaving one job. Me being here makes up for that a bit, don't you think?"

"You have an odd sense of logic."

*No more so than your husband's.* "I thought my logic might extend to you spending some time with me when you get home."

Piet focused on the hand I slid across the spare half of mattress. "You might not want to stay. Not when you've had to look after Nix for a few hours."

He disappeared out into the hall, leaving me to think through what he'd said. If this was a test, I was expected to fail. But I wasn't going to fail. If he wanted to change his mind about us, then he'd have to say so. I wasn't giving him any more ammunition.

"He's still sleeping," Piet said, coming back into the room. "Last chance to change your mind. I can risk calling in sick again."

"No need. I've got this." I could deal with any mood Nix might be in. He did, after all, seem to like me.

"Thanks." Piet offered an awkward smile then started off down the hall.

"Hey," I called after him. "What about my goodbye kiss?"

Piet returned to the doorway. "I thought you'd rather give that to Nix, since you couldn't get enough the last time you were here. Just bear in mind he has been chucking up for most of the day."

He was out the door before I'd even begun to formulate a response.

After he'd gone, I grabbed the remote. They didn't have a fancy TV. No Netflix or Sky. Just the basic channels. I skimmed through until I found something passingly watchable. I managed about thirty minutes of peace before the sound of a bell chimed off the walls.

I let it ring a couple of times to let him know I didn't intend to be at his beck and call. Not that he was expecting me, but I wasn't going to pander the same way Piet did.

At the third intrusive buzz, I forced a casual stroll to his room.

He lay in the center of the double bed, swathed in too many blankets and wearing an eye-mask which blinded him to my presence.

"What'd you want?" I asked, a bit too abruptly for someone who was playing nursemaid. But it wasn't as if I'd had any practice. Allowances would have to be made.

Nix shoved the mask to his forehead. "Why are you here?" His gaze homed in, squinty and mole-like. "Where's Piet?"

"He's left for work." I took a perch on the side of the bed. "I'm here by his invitation this time, so you should be pleased. What do you need?"

"Doesn't matter."

"Why'd you ring, then?"

His Adam's apple bobbed against the stubble-roughened skin of his throat. "I need the toilet."

"That's no problem." As long as he didn't expect me to hold it for him. I definitely wasn't wiping his arse. Under any circumstances.

"I can see what you're thinking." Nix blinked at me. "You only need to take me to the door. I can do the rest myself."

I tried not to let my relief show as I flicked back the edge of his blankets. "Can you walk? Or do you need carrying?"

"I don't know until I get up." He grabbed the covers like I might tear them from his vulnerable body. "Can't you call Piet? I'd rather he help me."

"He's on a trial. If you want him to lose his new job, I'll call him. Otherwise you got me making myself useful."

Nix lifted his chin. "I'm not a household chore."

"How desperate are you to take a piss?"

Nix clung to the blanket a couple of seconds more, then pushed them away. His slight body was half-drowned in a pair of light blue pajamas. "Help me sit up."

He was going to milk this for all he was worth, I could tell. I wasn't doubting he was ill—his pale skin and too-thin frame were clues enough—but couple that with a saber-sharp tongue and a demanding nature, and I was lumbered with the patient from hell.

I slipped one hand between his back and the pillow and the other on his upper arm. All I could feel were bones poking through the cotton. Fighting the urge to pull away, I remained steady as Nix shifted around and placed his bare feet to the floor.

"Wait." He trembled under my touch. "I need a minute."

I let him go. He slumped down, shuddering.

"How come you're so ill today when you were fine the other night?"

Nix raised his face. Two unnaturally bright spots of color sat high on his cheeks. "That was a good day. Most of my days aren't."

"Are you saying this is how you usually are?"

"Yes. I think I'll walk. It's more dignified."

*More dignified than being carried, presumably.*

I slipped his arm around the back of my neck, then my own around his hip. Bracing for us both to stand, I rose too quickly. He squeaked, lurched toward me, then promptly threw up.

"What the...?" I let go of him. More shoved him, really. As though he was a drunk who'd downed one too many whiskeys. "I thought you wanted the toilet." I looked down at the lumpy gruel splattering me from chest to belly. "You could've warned me."

Nix lay sprawled across the bed on his belly, face buried in the blankets. His feet skittered up the bed until the blankets completely absorbed him.

*He must be embarrassed.* I hadn't given much thought to his illness. I'd assumed he lay around all day looking superior and ethereal while being a right royal pain in the arse, but clearly there was more to it. He wasn't even drunk, and none of this was his fault.

I grabbed a blanket and tugged. Nix lay curled underneath. I caught the darker patch of blue streaking his inner thigh. The contents of his stomach weren't the only thing he'd lost.

"I don't need the toilet now," he said, confirming what I'd worked out for myself. "You can go."

I grabbed the sheet and used the corner to wipe the crud from my clothing. "I'm not leaving you like this." The raw stink of puke was making my stomach curdle. I gingerly removed my top and chucked it down in a heap with the blanket. The arid air clung to my bare skin, drying the sweat. "We're going to clean you up before Piet gets home. How about a trip to the shower?"

"No!" He made a grab for the blankets. "You're not seeing me naked."

I raised my hands, having momentarily forgotten all about his skin phobia. "How about I take you to the shower and wait outside the door while you get yourself sorted. I don't need to come in."

"No. Piet won't be long."

"He'll be hours. I'm not taking no for an answer."

Nix tugged the blankets to cover the darker wet patch staining the front of his pajama bottoms.

"What are you afraid of? I've seen guys naked before. Lots of them." Too many, if I started thinking on it. I didn't even know why the number should depress me, yet it did.

"But not me. You don't know me."

"No, but I know Piet. And I care about him enough to take care of you when needed."

"You care about Piet?" He tried to raise himself up on his forearms, but they failed to hold. He surrendered to the mattress, his hair falling across his face in a wispy web. "He's not yours to care about."

This was new. The first spear of jealousy. I could exploit this, see where it led. "He's been mine plenty over the past few weeks."

"Sex doesn't count."

"What if it was more?" It hadn't been, not for Piet, but I couldn't deny I wanted more than what I was getting.

"That wouldn't work." He swept the hair from his eyes. "Piet's mine. We're married."

"He could leave you any time he wanted."

"Not for you."

For a fleeting moment, I wondered if it might be possible. We had enough chemistry. I was the first man Piet had wanted in on this marriage. Or rather, to become a part of it.

"Maybe not me." I'd grant him the security he needed even if it was fake. "But someone. One day. Someone who doesn't lie in bed stinking of piss and puke because they won't be helped by anyone but the one person who needs the break every now and then."

Nix looked at me skeptically. "Are you saying all this so I'll do what you want?"

"Who knows? Your call. Wanna risk me being right?"

"You won't be right today."

"No, but when he gets back, he'd rather you were clean and comfortable. Wouldn't you rather be clean and comfortable for him, too?"

"I suppose so." He held out his eye-mask. "But you'll have to wear this."

"This isn't a good time to get your kink on."

"I'll need some help with the shower, and I don't want you looking at me."

Anyone else and I'd know they were on the wind-up. But he was completely serious. How would that work? I'd not only not see him, I'd not see the shower or anything else.

"Well?" He shook the mask. "You're the one who made all the fuss in the first place."

*Yeah, and now beginning to wish I hadn't bothered.* "I don't have to put that on until we get in there, do I?"

"Of course not. You might drop me. Or ram me into something."

In other circumstances, I might've rammed him into something all right. I stuffed the mask into the pocket of my jeans. "I take it I'm going to be carrying you in."

"I'm feeling dizzy, so you might as well." He lifted both arms toward me. "What are you waiting for? This was your idea."

*Not one of my better ones.* "Try not to throw up over me this time."

"If you're extra nice, I'll try not to pee on you, either."

"Are we back to the kink already?"

He lowered his arms. "What do you mean?"

The Kid was either too innocent for his own good, or that was what he wanted me to think. "Never mind." I braced a knee on the mattress. "Put your arms around my neck."

A mist of vomit and piss clung to my nasal hair as I lifted him up. Gritting my teeth, I got us both through the bedroom door and across the hall into the bathroom. I lowered him to the toilet seat while I went to sort out the shower.

"How does Piet handle the shower situation when you're ill?" I asked as I pulled the little seat from the wall.

"We usually shower together."

Nice idea, but he must know we weren't going to be doing that. Not with his 'naked body' phobia and especially not with Piet's unspoken order not to go near.

"I need to clean my teeth first."

I wondered, as I collected his toothbrush and loaded it up with paste, just how much a professional home help would get paid for taking care of someone like Nix. Whatever the amount, it wouldn't be enough.

"You'll have to wear the mask," he said, after he'd given his teeth a good scrub. "I can take off my own clothes."

"In the shower?

"Yes." He offered out his arms to be carried. The things I did for…whatever it was I was doing this for. Not Piet's approval, because he wouldn't. Approve. Not of me getting into the shower with his husband, even fully clothed and wearing a blindfold.

I settled him in the plastic chair, then pulled the mask from my pocket. "I can wait outside if you'd prefer. Now you're sat there safe and –"

"No. It's not safe. I might fall."

I slipped the mask over my head. "Do you want me to turn around as well?" I asked, when I couldn't see a thing.

"That won't be necessary." A rustle of clothing accompanied his voice. My hearing had picked up considerably.

"Are you getting naked?" I asked, a tad teasingly as I tried to home in on the thin outline of light around the mask.

"Yes." A touch of uncertainty laced his tone. "Why?"

"You're not much for humor, are you?"

"Did you say something humorous?"

"I guess not."

"Here." A whisper of cool air accompanied the flutter of cotton against my cheek. "That's the top."

"Are you talking about me? Or this?" I held up the pajamas to show him.

"I don't understand." He had to, even with the humor bypass. "You can switch the water on."

I wished I could switch myself off until Piet came home. Instead I felt around above Nix's head for the shower's On button.

Water jetted out, cold and fast enough to spatter my naked upper body with a full-on blast. I angled the head away from Nix until the water started warming. As I made to pull away, his fingers encircled my wrist.

He slipped something into my hand. A balled-up piece of netting. One of those sponge type things to wash with. "There's gel on the shelf above you. Piet always washes me."

*What, and now he expects me to do the same? Blindfolded? He doesn't mind me touching him, but he doesn't want me looking?*

I felt around and hit the gel. I popped the lid and squeezed some out into the netting. There was a name for it, but I'd be fucked if I knew what it was. Or wanted to know come to that.

A waft of lemon spiked the air. "You sure you want me touching you?"

"You're washing me. There is a difference."

But I'd still have to touch him to do it. I couldn't see a thing. I might accidently touch him someplace that would freak him the fuck out. *Why didn't I just leave him to stew in his own body fluids?*

I reached out, blindly seeking a safe part of him to stroke the netting over. A sharp tug on my arm unbalanced me. I toppled forward and powered into a warm, wet body and a warmer, wetter pair of lips.

His kiss was as powerful as before. The lack of strength in his muscle had no bearing on the forcefulness of his tongue as it plunged into my unsuspecting mouth. I should have fought him — it wasn't as if I couldn't. But the water was hotter than it should have been, and the fiery droplets seared my skin, ignited my blood. Instead of pushing back, I got sucked in. Lured by the fevered strength and his hand weaving through my hair and his roving tongue exploring every inch of my stunned mouth.

# Chapter Fifteen

Eventually, I realized the consequences of what amounted to an illegal kiss outweighed my arousal. My hands found Nix's shoulders and pushed. Our lips parted with a heartfelt squish.

"I thought you were having a bad day," I said, barely knowing if my voice carried above the solid thrum of water.

He said something I didn't catch, but there was no attitude behind the words.

I lifted one hand to find the dial on the shower.

The air rang dry in the resounding silence.

"Can I take the mask off yet?" I asked, reaching to remove the thing.

"No," Nix said, louder than he'd said anything since we got in the bathroom. "I'm still naked and you need to wash my hair."

I backed out of the cubicle, dripping all over the tiles. "Don't push your luck."

I unzipped my jeans. They were soaked through. "And don't go getting any ideas. I'm stripping because my clothes are wet. Not to give you cheap thrills." Peeling my jeans off wasn't much fun, and my pants beneath were just as wet. But no way was I removing those as well.

"You should have removed those before you got into the shower with me," Nix said, with a haughty sense of superiority, "then you wouldn't have wet clothing to dry off in the middle of the night."

I hadn't intended to get into the shower with him. He'd dragged me in with his kiss, though I'd do myself no favors by reminding him of that choice fact. Turning away, I hitched up the mask despite the ban. Then I grabbed the toweling robe hanging from a hook on the door.

I was all the way back to the shower cubicle before Nix noticed I wasn't wearing the mask.

"What are you doing!" He shrieked, then collapsed forward. Chest to thighs, arms wrapped around his knees. I'd only caught a glimpse of milky chest and a cluster of honey pubes, but there was nothing wrong with him. He wasn't thin to the point of cadaverous. He wasn't scarred or tattooed or any of those things I'd considered him having to hide.

"Why are you so freaked?" Kid would need counseling until he was fifty to recover from the trauma.

He sniffed, keeping his head to his knees. "I'm not fit or bluff like you."

"Bluff? As in blind man's bluff?" I offered him a rough estimation of a reassuring smile. "Haven't we played that game today?"

Nix raised his face. "Piet's pretty, and I'm not."

Where the fuck had he got that idea from? "You're as pretty as Piet," I said. "He must think the same, or why did he marry you?"

"Not for what I look like." Nix remained hunched over, staring at his feet. "I don't know if I can stand."

"Me looking at you?"

"No. Up."

I sighed. "How about we keep this nice and safe. Since you're so bothered about what I see and don't see, put the robe on back to front. That way I don't get to even accidentally peek at anything but your arse." When he hunched up even tighter, I offered him a smile. "This robe's big on you. If we tie the belt tight enough, you'll even be secure from me seeing that much."

Nix looked up. "You'll keep your eyes closed until I say you can open them?"

"Whatever." I'd had enough. I wanted out of this bathroom and into some dry pants. The alternative was strangling Nix with the robe's belt.

"Close them now. And bring the robe closer."

I gritted my teeth and did as I was told, almost wishing I'd made something important up when Piet had called and asked if I was busy this evening.

* * * *

"You can sleep in here with me." Nix flicked the corner of the clean blanket.

I'd finally managed to get him settled, after swapping the bedsheets for fresh ones while he was changing into a new pair of PJs in the bathroom. I'd put the linen in the washing machine along with my jumper and set the machine to wash and dry. So there was no way I'd be going home tonight, even if I wanted to. Not without clothes. The mattress had a wipe clean waterproof covering, which made me wonder if this wasn't the first accident Nix had had in this bed.

"You want me out of here that badly?"

"What do you mean?"

"I mean your husband virtually imploded when he found us sharing a bed the other night. What'd you think he'll do if he catches us snuggled up in his own bed tonight?"

"It's my bed as well." He pulled himself up against the headboard. "And he'll join us when he gets home. Take those damp underpants off and get in."

I made a theatrical gesture of pushing both hands against my junk. "What makes you think I want you to see me naked?" I wasn't sly on the sarcasm, but Nix remained deadly serious.

"I'll wear the mask." He took the thing off the bedside table where I'd dropped it in disgust. "Although I have seen you and touched you already."

I backed toward the door, hands still pressed to my cock. "It's safer if I take the sofa bed."

"How do you mean, safer?"

*He must know the answer. Why does this kid needed everything spelled out?* "Because, like I said, I don't want Piet getting the wrong idea."

"Do you want to have sex with me?"

I ran a hand through my hair and idly wondered if I survived as much as a week in Nix's company whether I'd be balding by the end of it. "About as much as you want to get naked."

"I'm not getting naked for you."

"There's the answer to your question." I moved to the doorway. "All right if I go get some sleep? Or are you going to ring your bell at me all night?"

He stared at me, all blankets and big eyes. "The bed will be warmer with you here, and when Piet gets home, he can join us. You can have sex with him for the rest of the night and completely ignore me."

I couldn't work out if there was any venom in his words. Did he really not give a shit about other guys getting intimate with his husband? Considering I was here, I guess he didn't. I should be thankful for that instead of uncomfortable. But the nagging suspicion that what I was doing was driving an even deeper wedge between an already troubled married couple refused to go away.

"Five minutes, then. Just until you're asleep." I returned to the bed and sat back against the headboard.

Nix was silent for the longest time. And the longer he was silent, the more I tensed. I just knew he wasn't done yet. The next question out of his mouth — and I could guarantee there was one on its way — would be a corker.

"Do you think it's possible to fix me?"

And there it was. The indecipherable beginning. "How do you mean?"

"With sex. Do you think you could make me like it? As much as Piet does?"

*How the fuck do I answer something like that? The only way I know how to, I guess. Badly.* "I don't think it would be in my best interests to make you like it. If you and him got it right together, that would make me redundant before we've even got this thing started."

"Yes. I never thought of that." He grew silent again, but I could almost hear the whirr of his thoughts. "Piet never much liked to put his penis into me."

"Right." A spark of interest shooed some of the grimness from the room. "Did you like it?"

"No. It hurt."

"It gets better," I said. "The more you practice."

He turned toward me. "Does Piet practice with you?"

He was asking if Piet had fucked me. I wished he'd stop probing, but since they were married, I guess he was owed.

"I'm not into receiving more than fingers or tongue up there." I'd never wanted to take like I gave. That was what guys like Piet were for.

"Would you like me to suck your penis?"

My breath actually caught. Like I shouldn't be getting used to these random grenades as far as Nix's conversation skills went. "Uh, no." I hesitated a touch too long. "I think I'm good. Thanks."

"Should I just go to sleep then?"

"I think that'd be best."

"Okay." He shifted closer, pressed his cheek to my shoulder and an arm across my chest.

He was warm. And he smelled, oddly, of lavender. And my dick processed that scent, reminding me how I'd just vetoed a blowjob from a beautiful, if peculiar, boy. I was just thinking about getting up and shifting back to the sofa bed, where I could take care of the hard-on throbbing in my pants, when a key twisted with an audible click in the front door.

Piet was home, and the first thing he'd see was my absence in the lounge. And once again I had no real excuse for being caught sharing a bed with his husband.

# Chapter Sixteen

A light went on in the hall and cast a thin strip of yellow under the door.

His footsteps paused outside and my heartbeat took over. Loud and thudding. I couldn't move. I still had Nix in my arms. If I were to wake him, he'd yelp.

A floorboard creaked. My muscles twitched. Nix remained a dead weight against me. A moment later, the footsteps resumed, tapping down the hall.

I lay rigid in bed, waiting for the shriek of despair once Piet realized I wasn't in the right bed. And that I hadn't gone home, because my jeep was parked outside. He couldn't have missed it on his way in.

When Piet didn't come bursting in, when the silence beyond the room got too much, I slipped away from Nix and ventured out of the bedroom door.

I found him outside, seated on the bench beneath the pallid scowl of a security light. A lit cigarette rested in his hand, though he made no attempt to set the filter to his lips.

"Nothing happened," I said. My lack of clothing undermined my line of defense, but I didn't think Piet would be such a heartless bastard as to boot me out in only my pants. Not once he'd let me explain. "Not how you think."

Piet chugged on the cigarette. A breath of smoke fumed on the breeze. "And what do I think?"

I hesitated. *Can't get this wrong. Not again.* "Well, any conclusion you might've jumped to when you saw I wasn't in the right bed." I could have told him I'd only popped to the bathroom. Until Nix opened his big mouth. Which he would, come morning. But I wasn't going to lie. I'd already decided that much. "First you should know that Nix threw up. Over me mostly, hence the lack of clothes." I gestured to my mostly naked body and didn't miss the way his gaze tracked my hand. "I thought he should take a shower." I wouldn't mention the piss. I'd allow the kid that much dignity. "Afterwards, we got talking. He asked me to stay until he fell asleep. I was about to go back to the sofa when you got home. It wasn't as if — "

"He let you see him naked?"

Was he finishing my sentences now? Because he'd got that wrong. When he looked at me, I realized this question was all his. Not only that, it also required an answer. I set a foot over the threshold. The chill of the paving slab cut through my sole, but I preserved and placed my other foot besides it. "I didn't see him naked. I had to wear this eye-mask thing." I took a couple of steps toward him. "Nix insisted."

Piet stubbed the cigarette out on the wooden tabletop. He lapsed into silence, which was worse than him ranting at me.

I took a perch on the other side of the bench. "I'm sorry." I itched to take the hand that rested on the table. I only resisted because I knew he'd walk if I touched him. "Nix wanted company. Not sex. But then, you know he doesn't want that."

"Not with me, anyway." Piet took out another cigarette from the pack on the table. My pack. As an afterthought, he offered the box to me. "Do you find him attractive? You didn't answer me the last time I asked."

It was a loaded question, impossible to answer in the right way. If I said yes, he'd explode with jealousy. If I said no, he'd be offended. On his own or Nix's behalf. Also, if I said the latter, it would make me a liar.

I took the offered cigarette, even though it was mine in the first place, and a light. "Do I find him physically attractive, or am I attracted to him?"

"Isn't that basically the same thing?"

I was stalling. And continued to stall when I sucked the smoke deep into my lungs. "If what you're really asking is do I want to fuck your husband, the answer is no." I looked up. "What I'd like to know is what it is you want."

"From you? Just the sex." He couldn't have made it sound any less meaningless. "I have everything else with Phoenix."

Did he, though? Even if that were true, Phoenix wasn't getting much of anything from Piet, and that was their problem. Neither of them seemed interested in sex with each other, and they didn't appear to discuss these things. Not together. "So why do I get the feeling all you want to do is push me away?"

Piet took another pull on his cigarette and spent a little longer than he needed to letting the smoke trickle from the corner of his mouth. "Because I'm afraid of what might happen if I stop."

*Me, too.* The only way this thing with Piet would end was badly. Yet I wasn't ready to walk. "You're a lot of work, you know that? You both are."

He met my gaze. "Then why are you still here?"

I detected the edge in his tone. I didn't know why it was there. All I was doing was trying to pay him a compliment. Or it was time I spelled it out.

"It's because I like you a bit, don't I?" I'd told him this, but I don't think it had sunk in. I wanted him to know before this whole arrangement went tits up. *Or in our case, balls down. Whatever.*

"How much is a bit?"

More than he'd like and more than I'd like. I couldn't tell him. I'd have to lie. I showed him my finger and thumb an inch apart. "This much."

Piet studied the space in between. "That's not much."

It also wasn't even a fraction of the truth. "Not enough to scare you off?"

"As long as like stays within the parameters of like, then no. I'm not scared by that." He smiled, just wide enough to warm me against the chill of a potential rejection.

"What happens now?" I leaned back now the air wasn't quite so tense. "Do I still get to stay, or…"

"I wouldn't try leaving dressed as you are. Not unless you fancy getting yourself arrested."

I matched his faint smile with a sixty-watt grin of my own. "Was hoping you'd say that."

"But you needn't think you're getting anything other than a few hours' sleep." Piet ground his cigarette into the table. "We haven't decided how any of this is going to work yet."

"That's something we could talk about now, if you like."

He shook his head. "I'm tired now. And Nix is in bed, so it'll have to wait until morning." He rose from the bench and made to head back inside.

I grabbed his wrist as he passed. "Hey."

He stopped. His hand formed a fist below my grip. "What?"

"Can I ask you something?"

"You don't usually ask. You usually just say it."

That was true. Even if he'd said no, I would have still voiced the question. "Why did you get married so young?"

The slight jerk of his muscles was the only indication of the question's impact. "Nix and I have always known we were going to spend our lives together. We've been sharing a bedroom since we were ten."

This was news. Big news. I'd had no idea they'd known each other that long. "How?"

"Our parents were together once. And no, we're not related by blood if that's going to be your next question."

It wasn't. They'd hardly be legally married if they were related. "Your folks split up?"

"Yes. And Nix and I wanted to stay together, so we got married. It made things easier for us to get a home together."

*They didn't marry out of love, then. Just for better circumstances.* "And you were always okay with not getting physical?"

"I've always accepted that Nix is how he is." Piet pushed at my shoulder with his free hand. "Can you let me go now? I'd like to go to bed."

He clearly wasn't going to volunteer any more information. I could see things getting awkward if I pushed, so I released him instead.

Piet started back toward the flat. He stopped in the doorway and looked back over his shoulder. "Are you coming?"

"Yeah." I reached for another cigarette. "In a minute."

I couldn't work them out. A couple of hours ago, Nix had kissed me with the same hunger as any man I'd ever kissed. Yet Piet would deny that Nix was capable of that level of emotion. No, not emotion. Piet would deny Nix a sexuality. That from the point of view of half a married couple was as weird as fuck. It was also nothing to do with me.

I sat out shivering until I finished my cigarette, then stubbed the end out on the bench before heading back inside.

The lamp was on. It hadn't been, earlier, when I'd headed outside. But now it was. The halo of light was more than enough to pick out the extra lumps and bumps under the covers. "What are you doing?"

Piet sat up. He had a T-shirt on, but I couldn't see if that was all he was wearing. The cover sat loosely across his hips. "I'm in bed. Where I told you I'd be."

"I didn't think you meant this one." I closed the door to keep out the chill of a midnight breeze. "Why aren't you with Nix?"

"I thought you wanted us to spend some time together."

"Right." I stayed where I was, unsure what to do next. "So you want to…"

"Oh. No." He fetched the covers to his chest. "I just want to share the bed. If that's okay."

"You mean this is a test to see if I can keep my hands to myself?"

"No." He sounded offended that I dare suggest that it was. "Nothing can happen until I've let Nix know. It's one of the rules. And he's asleep, so sharing the bed is the best I can do."

I stared at him. Made him wait. When he began to look uncertain, I barely managed to subdue my smile. I should have been pissed off that he had to ask permission whenever he wanted to fuck. But I wasn't. I thought it was...endearing. "Budge up."

Piet shifted to the other side of the bed. I slipped into the warm space he'd left and lay down. Almost immediately Piet curled his body around mine, pushing his face into my neck, the warm bulge of his cock pressed to my lower belly. I was disappointed to feel a thin covering of cotton against my thigh. He had his pants on, just as I was still wearing mine.

"I'm glad you're here," he said, his warm breath puffing against my neck. He smelled of toothpaste and soap. Fresh, clean, untainted.

"Are you?"

"Yes. We need you."

"Specifically me? Or just any old random you feel a passing attraction for?"

He lifted his head. "Any old random wouldn't have been any use to our marriage. Any old random wouldn't be able to fix us."

*Fix them?* The exact word Nix had used a couple of hours before, only about himself. Alarm bells? Yeah, I heard them. Battering my eardrums. Vibrating through my chest. My main purpose for being here was as a sticking plaster. Did they believe I could fix them? "I'm not sure it's a good idea to pin that kind of responsibility on me."

"I'm not." He pushed his cheek back to my chest. "I'm just saying that I'm glad you're here. You specifically, seeing as you insist on the clarification."

He didn't say anything else for a while. He seemed happy enough settled against me, and I had no intention of rocking the boat by asking any more awkward questions. Though I had a ton of them to be asked. Such as, if he and Nix had grown up together, why didn't they consider each other brothers rather than lovers?

I only had Nix's detailed version of their sex life to work with and I wasn't sure he was such a reliable source. So I kept quiet and waited for Piet to decide when it was time to go back to his husband.

# Chapter Seventeen

I woke to a shadow looming over the bed.

I blinked, and the shadow took form. Light, longish hair, voluminous flannel pajamas. A white-knuckled hand gripping a walking stick.

"I don't know why you've still got an erection," a loud voice announced. "You obviously had plenty of sex last night."

I looked down. The blanket I'd slept under was nowhere to be found. Neither was Piet. All I could see was my vibrant morning glory rising from my underpants. And Nix, standing above me. Less vibrant, but just as incessant.

"Where's Piet?" I gave my eyes a rub, then squinted at the kitchen. No, he wasn't there, either.

"He's in the shower."

What the fuck was Piet playing at, disappearing for a shower without waking me? The last thing I wanted was to have him see me like this. I sat up and ran a hand over my face. "Sorry."

Nix surveyed the crumpled sheet beneath me, possibly seeking evidence he wouldn't find. "I thought you'd be sleeping in our bed. Or am I to sleep alone from now on?"

My brain needed a shove into first gear. I scratched my head. "I won't be staying every night. Just occasionally."

"And on those nights, I'm to sleep alone?"

I scanned the crumped sheet on the other side of the mattress. "Piet didn't come to bed last night?"

"No. He was here with you. As you're more than aware."

I hadn't been aware. I'd assumed he'd disappear at some point to return to Nix. The fact that he'd actually stayed all night with me made me want to smile, but I managed to rein in the urge. For obvious reasons.

"Can you make pancakes?"

"Huh?" It really was too early for this. "Flour, water and…?"

"Eggs. I have lemon and honey on mine."

"On your eggs?"

Nix's solemn expression didn't falter. "On my pancakes."

"Right." He was asking me to cook him breakfast. "I should get dressed first."

"Yes. You wouldn't want to splash hot fat on your penis. Especially not in its erect state."

"No," I said. "I definitely wouldn't want that." I got up, feeling his eyes on me while I wandered around looking for my jeans. Then I remembered they were on the bathroom towel-rail where I'd put them last night to dry. And my jumper was in the washing machine.

*Let him look his fill. He's see it all anyway, as he was so keen to tell me the night before.*

"Are you planning to take him from me?"

"What?" Did he ever take a day off? My words from night were coming back to haunt me. "No. That was talk. No one will take Piet from you."

"Has he kissed you yet?"

"No. He hasn't kissed me."

Nix looked at me, as if seeking the lie that didn't exist. "I'll have two, so will Piet."

"Kisses?"

"Pancakes. But you'd better wash your hands first. As you also said last night, hygiene is very important."

Had I said that? I didn't remember.

"You're feeling better, then?" I asked as I made my way to the sink. "I mean, with you wanting two pancakes. And made by me, which is always a gamble."

"You said you could make them." Nix edged his way to the kitchen table with his stick and carefully lowered himself into a chair. "I don't see how that is a gamble. Unless you lied. Did you lie?"

"No." I knew how to make the damn pancakes. Didn't mean I knew how to make them well, but that was a complication I wasn't about to get into with him. "Tell me where everything is, and I'll get started."

"After you've washed your hands."

*Naturally.* I found some antibacterial hand wash on the window ledge behind the sink and pumped a generous dollop into my palm.

"I'll have tea, too," Nix said. "Green. Because today I am at home."

*Cute.*

I found a stray tea towel to dry my hands on, then made a show of displaying my hands, front and back to Nix for approval. "See? Totally germ free."

"Germs are invisible." Nix frowned at me—the blatant village idiot. "You are aware of that, aren't you?"

"Dirt free, then. Also, jizz free, pubic hair free and—"

"Dean!"

Of course, Piet had to choose that moment to walk in, fresh and damp-haired from his shower.

"I'm making pancakes," I said. "Nix was checking my hands are clean."

"Why are you making pancakes?" Piet fixed me with a wary eye from behind his glasses as he drew out the other chair at the table. "And where are your clothes?"

"Around. Somewhere. Nix asked me to cook."

"He's very rude," Nix said, placing me firmly back in the tense of second-person present. "I think he wanted sex this morning, and he's upset because he didn't get any."

"I'm not upset," I said, barely managing to unclench my jaw. "I'm just..." They were both looking up at me from the table, like my explanation was everything. *Fuck it.* "I'm trying to make breakfast before I head off to work. Is that okay with the two of you?"

"He hasn't got very far." Nix turned to Piet. "I've asked for tea, but he hasn't even filled the kettle yet."

"I'm working on that," I said. "Why don't the two of you go back to bed? I work better without an audience."

"I'm not an audience." Nix folded his arms. "And I've only just got up."

"Ever heard of breakfast in bed?"

"Yes, I have. Because that's what I have every morning. Until today. Because today Piet was too busy sharing the sofa bed with you to bother cooking for me."

"That isn't true," Piet said, and for once I was glad not to be his sole focus of attention. "I was going to make breakfast when I'd finished my shower."

"Well. You were too late. Dean's making it now. Practically naked."

He clearly didn't appreciate my state of undress. "Fine." I set down the eggs. "I'll go find my clothes."

I left the room, with not quite the finesse I might've had if Nix hadn't scuffed the shine from my mood. Not for the first time, I considered what exactly was in this for me. Piet, but only on a part-time basis. But if the alternative was no Piet, I'd learn to accept Nix's moods. *Somehow.*

My jeans were still on the bathroom towel rail. Still damp and cold and not the most comfortable against my skin. But they'd have to do, since I hadn't brought a change of clothes and neither Piet's nor Nix's stuff would fit me. But then I wouldn't be seen dead in anything from Nix's wardrobe.

I started back down the hall, ready to give Nix a twirl in my damp jeans, when I stopped just shy of the doorway.

"Why are you so upset about it?" Piet asked from the kitchen. "You wanted me to share a bed with Dean."

"Only to have sex. Not to spend the entire night with him and leave me on my own."

So much for jealousy not being an issue. And if it became an issue for Phoenix, it'd be an issue for Piet. And — all importantly — me.

"I've got a day off at the end of the week." I breezed back into the room, like the air wasn't as fragile as the eggshells I was about to crack. "How about we all go out?"

"Where?" Nix asked, clearly unimpressed. Whether with me or the thought of us all going out together, I didn't know.

"The beach. You two got Speedos?"

Nix exchanged a look with Piet. They were both wearing the same frozen expression. I might as well have invited them on the annual naturist tour of Chernobyl.

"Nix doesn't like the beach." Piet got up. He moved to a cupboard and pulled out a small frying pan. "His skin is very sensitive. And he can't swim."

"We don't have to go to the beach. We could go for a meal. I know a couple of nice pubs out in the country."

"Nix and I don't have money to waste on overpriced pub lunches." Piet grabbed a bag of flour from the cupboard. "Why are you so eager to take us out?"

These kids had nineteen-year-old bodies under sixty-year-old heads. This was going to have to change. "I want to get to know you. We can do things together other than fuck, can't we?"

"I knew it." Nix slapped a palm down on the table. "You did have sex last night."

"No, we didn't." Piet blew out a breath. "I've told you nothing happened."

Nix's lips tightened. "But you'd rather share a bed with him than me. And the beach. Don't bother denying that you want to go. I can read it in your face."

"I'd only go for an hour or so. Would you be all right to look after yourself, or…?"

"There's no need for me to stay home." Nix sat up straighter in his seat. "I'll be better by the end of the week."

"But you don't like the beach," Piet said, and there may have been a hint of resentment there.

"Just because I didn't like it with you doesn't mean to say I won't like it with Dean." There was so much more to read in that sentence that I couldn't begin to formulate a response. Nix raised his gaze. "What time are you going to collect us, exactly? Because Piet will need to wash my hair first."

# Chapter Eighteen

Beachwear for Nix consisted of a pair of white-framed sunglasses with mirror lenses, a wide-brimmed straw hat with a purple ribbon tied around the base, a close-fitting *My Little Pony* T-shirt baring half an inch of slender midriff, cropped jeans two sizes too big and jelly shoes complete with an actual heel. He topped this off with a blob of sun cream slathered over his nose.

Piet wore jeans and a thin gray sweatshirt that may have at one time or another been black. He came along armed with a rucksack he said was filled with sandwiches, crisps and fruit squash. I also caught him sneaking a towel and some sun tan lotion in there, too. Which meant he wasn't going to need much, if any, persuading to get into the water.

They both looked about as comfortable as a couple of penguins in Barbados, but we were going out. Together. Like we made up three thirds of a fully working polyamorous relationship.

"This ancient old thing?" Nix exclaimed, when I presented him with my jeep at the curbside. He spoke as if he'd be expected to thrust his feet through the floor and run until we hit the top of the hill.

"Hey, show some respect. This baby is older than you." I gave the passenger door a pat. "I bought her as a non-runner from a scrap yard when I was seventeen. Done her up and she's never let me down yet."

Nix surveyed me through the shadow of his hat. "It's a car. Not a person. Why haven't you got something new? Even Piet's car is younger than this."

"Because I love this car. Take enough trips to the beach with me and you'll learn to love her, too."

"I'm sitting in the front," he said, haughty as a queen. "That part has a solid roof."

"Be my guest." I opened the door. He eyed me warily before venturing, very delicately, inside.

"Hope you're good with sitting in back," I said to Piet as I shut the door with Nix safely inside.

It was clear to me that if any trousers were being worn in this relationship, they firmly belonged to Nix. Not that Piet was in any way a timid soul in the bedroom, but in day to day living, I didn't think he got to be number one in anything.

"You want some music?" I asked, when we were on our way and no one seemed interested in conversation.

"No." Nix looked over at me from the passenger seat. "Can this heap go faster than twenty-five?"

We were in a thirty limit. "Wait until we're on the open road. I'll blow your hat off."

"Now there's a promise I don't suppose you'll bother to keep."

I looked over at him as he stared through the windscreen ahead. Somehow, I didn't think he was talking about the drive.

As soon as we were out of town, I whipped the jeep around the tight curves and banged the throttle to the floor. The fields and the farms and the country pubs and the public footpaths breezed past as I focused on giving Nix what was probably the first thrilling ride of his life, and the only kind I was ever likely to take with him.

I was concentrating so hard on the road I didn't hear Piet until he started hammering on the back of my seat. "Please, just slow the hell down!"

I eased my foot off the accelerator. "Sorry." I threw a glance over my shoulder. "Got a bit carried away."

I looked at Nix and found him bright eyed and pink-cheeked. He wasn't smiling, as if he ever did, but his mouth was slightly open and his breath escaped in fast, even little puffs.

"Was that fast enough for you, Mr. Speed Demon?" I asked, flashing him a grin.

Nix must've realized his excitement was written all over his face because he immediately shut down again, concealing any hint of what he was actually feeling. "It was quite fast," he said with a superior air, "but not fast enough to blow my hat off." He pinched the brim. "See how it's still sitting very firmly on my head."

I could see that. I could also see the first bit of color in his cheeks, cheeks that were usually ashen. "Let's see what we can do about that on the way back."

"Can you please just keep within the speed limit?" Piet glared at me in the rear-view mirror.

I slowed a little more. "I can try."

"Piet doesn't like to do anything fast," Nix announced, although his accusation wasn't quite true. Because Piet liked to fuck fast. Too fast sometimes.

I took them to an out of the way beach under a cliff. No amenities except a car park and an ice-cream van. I thought they'd appreciate the privacy. As it turned out, there were quite a few other people who thought the same, which rendered the place not quite so secluded as it might have been on a less sunny day.

Nix chose the spot where we had to sit. A space set back slightly into the cliff, which might've lent us that touch of privacy if not for his garish hat and glittery shoes.

Both he and Piet seemed oblivious to the less than furtive stares we'd collected walking across the shingle, so I pretended I hadn't noticed, too. Piet laid out the towels, then produced one of those inflatable pillows and proceeded to blow into it.

Nix managed to sit down without assistance and flung off his girly shoes with abandon. His dainty feet were as pale as the few inches of leg beneath his cut-offs.

"They won't fit you. Your feet are far too big."

I looked up to find Nix staring at me.

"Shame," I said, fighting hard not to come back with a line of sarcasm Piet definitely wouldn't approve of.

Piet had stripped down to a pair of long, baggy swim shorts. Just a glimpse of his freckled skin was enough to kick-start a fantasy not appropriate for a family-filled beach.

He produced a bottle of sun lotion, which he promptly handed to Nix, then sat on the towel with his back to Nix and his front to me. When Nix started rubbing sun cream into Piet's shoulders with a generous massaging motion, my cock jolted behind my fly. The two of them might not touch each other sexually, but my ragingly horny imagination supplied a variety of positions these two might get themselves tangled up in. There wasn't a hope in hell of reining in my inappropriate thoughts.

Nix peered at me from over Piet's shoulder. "What's he looking at us like that for? Again."

I forced myself to turn from the intimate show they had no idea they were putting on and started undressing.

"Here." Piet offered me his sun cream. "You'd better use this."

I didn't take the bottle. "I don't need any help from the factor twenties."

"It isn't about tanning," Nix said snottily. "It's about protecting yourself from the UVAs and Bs."

"Tell me something I don't know." All I got by way of reply was a blank stare from Piet and an approximation of the same from Nix behind his mirrored lenses.

"Sit down." Piet gestured to the shingle in front of him. "I'll do it, then we know it's done properly."

My objection died in my throat. Piet was offering to put his hands on me. All the places not covered by cloth. I dumped myself down where he'd indicated. Piet hadn't touched me much, but his palms had rested on my chest often enough that I knew what to expect.

His hands, cool with cream, wafted over my shoulders and ignited my cock. I grabbed my rolled-up towel and pressed it to my groin, lest we start attracting more unwanted attention than we already were.

"Look. He's trying to hide yet another erection."

I opened my eyes, only now realizing I'd closed them. "If you're talking about me," I said, throwing a look at Nix, "I'm a hot-blooded twenty-three-year-old-guy. It would be strange if I didn't get a hard-on, don't you think?"

Nix lay back onto his inflatable pillow and raised a book to his face. *Fifty Shades*. Nothing this kid did surprised me anymore.

"I'm not doing this to turn you on, pervert." Piet poked me above my right kidney. It was a good-natured poke, and my dick responded accordingly. "You can do the rest yourself." He tossed the bottle between my legs and moved away.

*Bloody Nix and his machine-gun gob.* I missed the heat of Piet's palms. I opened the cap and started applying more cream, less than half-heartedly, to my chest and belly.

"Right. I'm going in." Piet started picking his way down the shingle.

I wasted no time in slinging the bottle of sun cream at Nix, then getting to my feet to chase after him.

"Too cold for you?" I asked, coming to stand beside him. The water barely tickled his calves. He stood with both arms glued around his waist. The water held a certain bite despite the power of the sun beating down on our near-naked bodies.

"Why is it never as warm as it looks?" Piet asked, through chattering teeth.

"It's fine once you're under." I waded a step or two past him. "Fancy racing me out to those yachts over there?" I gestured to where a few boats bobbed lazily about on the breeze.

Piet's mouth fell open. "I can't swim that well."

"But you're planning on doing more than standing here shivering 'til you hit quicksand?" I took a couple more steps into the water, gritting my teeth at the cold cutting up through my bones.

"Why don't you show me how it's done, then?" he said. I was standing ahead of him now and couldn't see his face. I could imagine his expression. Dark, with a hint of sly.

I threw myself into the icy water with a thrusting belly flop.

There was sound above. A voice, beating down, vibrating through the water. Next thing I knew I was being half-dragged, half-pinched to the surface.

I gasped in a mouthful of warm air, the chill of the water momentarily freezing my lungs. I squinted at the pale figure next to me.

"What?" I focused on his mouth moving harshly, making sound, trying to work out what he was saying with the water sloshing in my ears.

"...like a fucking idiot!"

I wiped the remainder of the water from my eyes. "What've I done now?"

"I thought..." His voice ran out of steam. "You didn't come back up for ages."

I hadn't been under for more than a moment. Piet had walked in to his chest to rescue me, which was thoughtful and cute considering how much he'd loitered in the shallows.

"You waded all the way out here to save my life?" I couldn't hide a grin despite the chill of the water.

"No. I waded out here to drown you for being a dick."

"Come out here and be a dick with me."

Piet stayed where he was, arms around his waist, trying to grip heat while his teeth chattered and his nipples hardened to acorns. "It's too cold for me."

"Want me to warm you up?"

He looked around. "In front of all these people? I don't think so."

If that was his only reason for turning me down, I'd warm him up later. Back at the flat, if he'd let me. "It's warmer when you get under. And this spot right here." I swum out another meter. "Where the sun's shining, it's as warm as the Med."

Piet eyed me, his arms folded around himself as he trembled. "You're such a bad liar, Dean Garner."

I relaxed back and floated on the water. The idea was to make myself look tempting enough he'd come out here and join me, which he'd do if he wanted to spend the time with me as much as I did with him.

When a bite of heat nipped at my foot, I raised my head. The glow pulsing through my chest was enough to turn the water warm as the Med.

Piet floated next to me, so rigid I was surprised he hadn't sunk straight to the bottom. I still enjoyed his closeness. Out here, despite the people milling about the beach and in the water, I felt as though we were alone.

# Chapter Nineteen

I encouraged Piet to swim beyond everyone else, just out of my depth and a way out of his. I held on to him while he wrapped both arms around my neck and set his cheek to my shoulder. His warmth radiated through my hands. His laughter caressed my ears. A laugh I'd never heard before. Not properly. Because he didn't, any more than Nix smiled. How they could both seem so content, yet in other ways so miserable with each other was beyond me.

We stayed that way, close in the water, me supporting us both, even when my strength ebbed. The feel of holding him in my arms was something new, which I intended to savor.

I breathed his salty-wet hair and stroked his cold, smooth skin under the water. Closing my eyes, I blocked out the screams and chatter of the people around us and transported myself and Piet a million miles away to our own private beach in our own private sea.

It didn't last, maybe because of my solid cock pushing against his thigh despite the chill of the water. Piet squirmed out of my arms, muttering about going to check on Nix.

We'd been in the water barely twenty minutes.

"I'm trying to read," Nix said, when we both turned up to ruin his fifty shades of whatever the hell he was getting out of that book. "Why are you interrupting?"

Piet stood there, indecision clearly working through him. He'd come to check on his ill husband, and yet here was the husband not wanting the interruption and making him feel lousy in the process.

"Because it's time for lunch." Piet gestured at the rucksack. "We're all hungry."

Nix raised the book in front of his face. "I'm not."

Such an obnoxious shit, but I knew better than to voice my opinion. I grabbed Piet's towel off the shingle and placed it around his goose-pimpled shoulders.

"I'm starving." I reached for my towel. "Can't wait to get stuck into those...what are we having?"

"Marmite sandwiches." Nix lowered his book. "That's what we always have for lunch."

"Not this time." Piet opened the rucksack. "We're having cheese. With bananas for afters."

Nix rolled onto his side, away from us, taking his book with him. "In that case, I'm definitely not hungry."

I spread my towel out and sat down. "What's wrong with him?"

"Nothing." Piet started unpacking the food. "That's just how he is."

If being 'just how he is' meant acting like an immature, precious little shit, then I didn't see why Piet had to put up with that behavior, husband or not.

"Here." Piet offered me two thin slices of droopy brown bread wrapped in cling film.

I took the sandwich, quite touched that he'd thought of me and packed lunch for three rather than two. "Thanks."

He'd been full of laughter a few minutes before. A young, carefree guy just out to enjoy himself. Now his frown had returned, lines etched across his forehead too deeply for a kid of his age.

He set out two sets of sandwiches on the picnic rug along with three plastic cups and a bottle of lemonade. Presumably, the bananas would make their grand appearance later.

Tragically sweet, the way he cared for someone who assumed that was his sole role in life. Or sweetly tragic. I couldn't decide which.

Was Nix jealous after all? Of me and Piet, out there in the water getting close? We hadn't kissed, but I'd had my hands all over him. Nix hadn't appeared to be watching us on the one or two glances I'd shot his way, but who was to say what went on under that broad sunhat and those dark glasses?

"What are you thinking about?"

I stopped chewing. Piet was studying me from the other side of the rucksack.

"Just contemplating another dip in the water if you fancy joining me."

Piet opened his mouth, but it was Nix's voice that bit the air.

"You have to wait an hour after you've eaten, or you'll drown."

"What? That's bullshit."

Nix rolled over. He set his book down and rather painfully, with a bit of teeth-gritting, sat up. "It's not.

Cinder told us if you swim on a full stomach, you'll get a cramp and you'll drown."

"Your drug-dealing mother is the fount of all medical knowledge, is she?"

"Dean." Piet looked at me, mouth agape.

"What? It is bullshit. Even if it wasn't, it only applies to kids." I took another big bite of the sandwich I wasn't enjoying but would eat because Piet had made it for me.

"Cinder is not a drug dealer." Nix snapped his book shut and tossed it to the shingle. "Just like you're not a prostitute just because you supply half your holiday park with sex. Or are you?"

Piet looked at me. Nix did, too, and I suddenly wished I was back in the water, floating with Piet. Just the two of us. Alone.

"Anyone for a banana?" Piet reached into the bag and pulled out a bunch of three.

\* \* \* \*

At some point during the afternoon, Nix wanted an ice cream. Which meant walking back up to the carpark. Before Piet could rummage around for change in his rucksack, I pulled a tenner from my jacket pocket.

"My treat," I said, getting to my feet.

"No. I've got money." Piet rummaged deeper in his bag.

"So have I. And you made up the picnic, so let me get the ice cream. What does everyone want?"

"Piet can go." Nix swiped the money from my fingers. "He's spent more than enough time with you." He thrust out the note toward his husband and didn't lower his arm until Piet had reluctantly accepted.

"I want to make a deal," Nix announced, once Piet was out of earshot.

"What deal?" I asked, only vaguely hearing him. My attention was very nailed to Piet's retreating arse.

"I want you to know that I won't be any trouble for the rest of the day."

"That's...good." What else was there to add? I should have insisted on giving Piet a hand with the ice creams. That was the only way he and I would get to spend some time alone.

"Yes. Which means you can spend that time having sex. With Piet."

I finally pried my attention from Piet's arse. Nix was studying me from behind his glasses. Had he actually been reading my mind? "You serious?"

"Yes. And in return, I want the same."

"The same what?"

"As Piet has."

*Okay, I'll bite. Or nibble.* "What, exactly, does Piet have?"

Nix's brow dropped. So did his voice. "Sex. Obviously. However he takes it."

I tried to take a calming breath, but this latest grenade of his was nuclear. I could only hope he was winding me up. Except for the part where he really didn't do that kind of thing. "With me?"

"As I have already stated."

"Does Piet know about this?"

"Of course not. He wouldn't like it."

*No shit he wouldn't like it.* I wasn't too keen on the idea myself. "I thought sex wasn't your thing."

"I need it to become my thing. Then I can make Piet happy. The way he is around you."

*Wow.* Had Piet been any different with me today than he was with Nix at home? He had frowned less today. He didn't frown in bed. Not unless I did something he didn't want me to do. Like touch him. Or kiss him. Or admit to liking him.

"You know it's you who Piet loves, right? He wouldn't be happy if you had decided to stay home. All he'd be thinking about is you. Me, I'm just a distraction." A distraction from the tedium of his everyday life, and because he wasn't getting any under-the-sheet activity from his husband.

Nix looked at me through his mirrored lenses. "Why don't you kiss him? When you were in the water, I could tell you wanted to."

"Do you want me to kiss him?"

"No. I want you to kiss me."

Maybe I should have expected a line like that, but I hadn't. Hadn't realized until now that Nix was in a strop because he was jealous and not just because he delighted in being an obnoxious pain in the arse. Jealous of his own husband rather than jealous of me, which was how it should have gone.

The most I could come up with was, "Why?"

"Because kissing's what I'm good at." He straightened at the prideful boast. "Plus, I like the feel of your tongue in my mouth. Do we have a deal? About tonight. You need to tell me now."

"What, about kissing you?" I could do that. Even here and now and sod what anyone else thought. Except Piet. I wouldn't want to risk contact in front of him when he and I had never kissed.

"No. About having sex with me."

Across the shingle, Piet was rapidly trotting toward us, armed with three ice creams. Two vanilla and one strawberry, the strawberry one loaded with all the sugary treats the van had on offer.

I made to push up from the shingle. "We'll have to discuss this later."

"No. Now." Nix's fingers clamped down hard on my thigh, pushing me back down again. "Or I will be very difficult this afternoon and you'll have to go home. I might be ill for days, so you won't be able to visit Piet for a very long time."

This was a side I hadn't seen before. I didn't know how I felt about it, either. Disgusted or intrigued.

When I checked on Piet, heading toward us with a curiously tight expression on his face, I knew that this was a conversation best saved for later.

For now, I gave him his answer. It was the simplest way to keep myself out of immediate trouble.

"Fine. Have it your way. Whatever."

I guess I convinced him, because his cool fingers left my thigh. I sprang up from the ground and hurried to help Piet with the ice creams. Anything to end this conversation.

I had no intention of going through with this little deal he'd invented. He deserved to be conned for being a devious bitch, but at that moment I couldn't see beyond having Piet to myself for the rest of the afternoon.

# Chapter Twenty

Back at the flat, Nix headed off for a lie down just as he'd said he would. Piet went along, too, presumably to help him into his pajamas, which was in no way a code for anything other than exactly what it was. I waited on the sofa, wondering if I could summon the courage to tell Piet about the conversation I'd shared with Nix while he'd gone for ice creams. Or, rather, the conditions Nix had set down. Whichever way I explained that to Piet, our afternoon would be over.

I would get around to telling him. At some point. Like, just before I went home with no intention of giving Nix what he thought he wanted.

"What are you thinking about?" Piet appeared in the doorway, cheeks pink as his nose despite all the sunscreen. He was still in his shorts and T-shirt from the beach, slightly damp and speckled with sand. To me, he'd never looked sexier.

"Just mulling over how we might fill the afternoon." I stretched out my legs. "Any suggestions?"

"Actually, I do." He beckoned me down the hall. I didn't need any further encouragement.

He ushered me into the bathroom and leaned back against the closed door.

"I thought we could both use a shower."

"Together?" Not that I had any objections, but this seemed a bit sudden. "With Nix across the hall?"

"He's got his earplugs in." Piet ripped off his T-shirt, then pulled down his shorts. "I'm showering, whatever. You can go and watch TV if you don't feel like joining me." He climbed into the cubicle and switched the water on.

*What are the choices again? Showering with Piet or daytime weekend TV?*

I didn't take a moment to fling off my clothes and join him. As Piet had said, Nix had his earplugs in.

Piet turned around and squinted up at me through the stream. Anyone else and I would've leaned in for a kiss. But kissing wasn't what we did, and I still wasn't sure I had permission to touch.

When his fingers brushed mine, I looked down. He pushed a condom into my hand, which left me in no doubt as to what he wanted. But still, I had to ask.

"You sure?"

"Nix and I have discussed it."

*They had? When?* Probably in the bedroom while I was twiddling my thumbs on the sofa wondering how and when I should break the news about Nix's plans for the evening ahead.

"You assumed I'd be up for it, then?" I asked, because I had to feign a semblance of autonomy.

Piet's warm grip closed around my cock. My shaft spasmed under his fist. "You're always up for it."

"True."

He reached up with his free hand and stroked my cheek. I wasn't sure what to make of this. It was far more intimate than the fist gripping my dick.

Up until now he'd only ever laid his hands on me sparingly, and purely for sex. Never with affection. This felt affectionate. Warming, even. Couples touched each other this way. Or I assumed they did. My experiences were limited.

Just as suddenly as he'd touched me, he turned away and pressed both palms flat to the tiled wall.

I scanned his reddened, freckled shoulders, and trekked a finger down the valley of his spine, before sliding an arm round his belly. I nestled my cock between the rounded curves of his arse.

"It'll hurt," I told him, on the off chance he wasn't aware. "If we don't use lube."

"I know. But do it anyway."

*No problem.* I placed the condom between my lips to keep it safe, then reached between his arse cheeks with my free hand. His little knot was all clenched and sealed against my wet fingertip.

He'd let me do this for him before, back at the park, on a couple of occasions when he was feeling generous or just relaxed enough. He'd never yet been relaxed enough to let me kiss him, though I was forever hoping that might change.

When I breached him, he gasped and steadied himself against the wall. I curled my fingertip inside him, seeking that special place that made him yelp and cry as enthusiastically as an adult movie star.

The first brush across his prostate, and the shock seemed to catch him off guard. His elbows gave way, almost making him trip. His body trembled under the gushing water. I pulled out my finger, barely giving him time to acknowledge the withdrawal before adding another, denying him the luxury of the gentle stretch.

I twisted them inside him, seeking to loosen the clenched muscles. Piet shivered. I felt the vibration all the way up my arm.

"Deannnn." His voice was a long whine of impatience, almost drowned in the thunderous stream.

I pulled my fingers from his body, then ripped the condom packet open with my teeth.

I was already hard. It didn't take much more than Piet's naked body to pull out a winning performance from me. His responsiveness when it came to sex was like no one I'd had before. Each time we were together, it was different. This being the most different so far.

I rolled the condom over my dick, then lined up to his delicious center. Piet obligingly angled his body, but he was still too tight.

I gripped his hip with one hand and nudged my dick in another inch. Fire sparked down my shaft and exploded in my lower belly.

Piet peered back at me, mouth open, water pouring down his face, plastering his hair to his head. "Keep going."

I had every intention of doing so.

"Like this?" I clamped my fingers around both his hips and plunged, forging through the tight resistance and halfway to dissolving in the pleasure rocketing through my body.

Piet yelped. His balance wavered, but I held him steady until he righted himself again. "Do it like that again." He shifted his legs farther apart. "But harder."

*Forever the boss.*

The water thundered down, stinging my skin. I gasped for air, adrenaline and arousal making my balls burn with the urge for release. My fingers bit into the sparse flesh of his hips and, when I let go with one hand to reach for his swollen cock, there were red marks left behind.

He offered no objection when I started jerking him off. Piet worked himself back against me, meeting my every thrust. A low groan bled from his lips in a steady pulse.

The first tingle of orgasm gathered to a fiery whirlpool in the pit of my belly. A louder cry burst from Piet's lips. He flung himself back against me, narrowly missing my teeth with the rear of his skull. His cum hit the tiles in thick, eager spurts, his channel clenching my cock as I held him steady in my arms.

I guided him back to the wall and resumed fucking him with the same solid thrusts. He was softer inside now, and my hips drove my lust until my skin prickled with the rapid approach of release.

I buried my face in his shoulder and bit down gently. Piet squirmed and thrust his backside against me. The overwhelming pressure squeezed too tightly. My release tumbled over me, as torrid as the shower jets. I clung to Piet for support, gasping for air.

Beyond the steamed-up shower door, something shifted. I turned my head to the right. Through the glass, I made out a ghostly figure. Pale and dressed in white. Staring at me as I was staring right back at him.

"Shit." I pulled out of Piet and almost toppled backward.

"What?" Piet regarded me though the shower stream. "What's the matter with you?"

I gestured to where he could see for himself what the matter was.

Piet reached past me and opened the shower door. "What am I looking at?"

There was nothing to see but an open bathroom door. A door that had been closed when we'd got into the shower. It was also a door with no lock, which meant anyone could have waltzed in. Anyone as in Nix, who could have been gawping at us for any length of time.

Piet switched the shower off. He stepped from the cubicle and grabbed a towel from the rail. There was only the one, which meant I was going to have to drip dry until he was done.

"I hope you're happy." His cock jiggled as he briskly rubbed the towel across his skin. "Spoiling the moment for no reason."

I wasn't happy. Far from it. And he should know why. "Nix was in here."

The towel dropped from Piet's fingers. "What?"

"I only saw him for a moment. When I looked again, he was gone."

"I don't know if you've noticed, Dean, but Nix doesn't move that fast. Are you sure you saw him and not a shadow?"

"Since when were shadows white? What was he wearing to bed?"

"Oh…hell." Piet snatched the towel off the floor and pushed it at me. "I'd better go see him."

"You reckon you should put some clothes on first?"

He glanced down at his naked body. "Oh. Yes." He started gathering his clothes off the floor. "How long had he been standing there?"

I set about dealing with the condom still attached to my spent dick. "No idea. I wouldn't have thought for long." I would have felt him watching a lot sooner if he'd been there the entire time. Or that was what I told myself as I launched the condom down the toilet.

"It's not as if he didn't know what was going to happen," Piet said as he threw his clothes on. "He said he'd stay in the bedroom."

"Maybe he was curious." I knew for a fact he was, but Piet didn't. I would tell him all about it. Just…after I'd dressed.

"He's curious about you. Never about me."

Another blade of jealousy. From him now rather than Nix. The two of them confused the hell out of me, but that was a part of the attraction. When would I ever have time to get bored?

"Get dressed." Piet picked up my clothes from the floor and dumped them in my arms. "Make yourself a coffee. This won't take long."

"You want me to stick around?" I hadn't thought he would. I'd expected him to blame me for Nix's impromptu voyeurism.

"Don't you want to?"

"Yeah, I want to." The fucking was only part of the plans I'd imagined for us this afternoon. Talking was a large proportion, too. We hadn't done nearly enough of that.

"I just need to explain the boundaries to Nix."

*Boundaries?* I didn't think Nix would take to those. But I wasn't going to agree to an audience. Not even if that audience was Nix.

Piet padded across the hall and into the bedroom while I dried off and dressed in my stuff from the beach. Clothes that were as gritty and damp as the atmosphere.

He returned when I was halfway through a cup of black coffee, his face solemn. My heart dipped toward my stomach. I knew before he said anything that he was going to kick me out. I set the mug down on the side table and rose. "Don't tell me. You think I should leave."

"Why would you think that? Because you knew Nix was going to tell me all about the sex you two were going to have tonight?"

It had crossed my mind. But the way Piet spoke made the whole bargain sound a lot worse than what it was. Especially because I had no intention of holding up my end, so to speak. And it had been entirely Nix's idea in the first place.

"I wouldn't have gone through with it," I said, and most of the way believed it too. "I just agreed so I could spend some time with you."

"Well, it doesn't matter now anyway. Because it's off." He came and took a seat at the other end of the sofa. "Seeing us in the shower has shattered his illusions."

"I take it that's not a good thing."

Piet shook his head. "He said it was the most horrendous display he's ever had to witness."

"Hey!" I straightened my shoulders. "We didn't invite him to the matinee. He must've known where we were and what we'd be doing."

"He said he was curious. Because of the..." Piet cleared his throat. "...noise I was making."

That made me smile, thought it was gone before Piet could see and get himself all offended. "You do tend to be quite vocal."

Piet lowered his head. "Do I?"

"Yep." I could sense his smile, even if I couldn't see it. Piet wasn't sacking me off. Not completely. I could live with that.

He sighed. "I thought all this was sorted. I thought he was okay with us."

I could have told him different. Had tried to on a couple of occasions. But he knew there was an issue now, and things would even out once they'd talked. And I wasn't needed for that. "We knew this wasn't going to be easy."

"You don't mind, do you? I mean about me kicking you out so I can sort things with Phoenix?"

"I'm not getting booted out, though, am I?" I rose from the sofa and started for the door. "I'm leaving voluntarily."

Piet's footsteps padded down the hall behind me. "I'll call you. You do know that, don't you?"

"Even if it's only to dump me?"

"I'm not going to…" He stopped talking. We both knew I was the expendable one and that there were no guarantees, no matter what we wanted. Nix was the only one who mattered, but Piet seemed keen that I know I meant something to him. Keener than he'd ever been before, anyway. "Just a moment." Piet unhooked a key on the wall by the door. "Take this. The code to the front door is on the keyring. Don't lose it."

Was he having a joke at my expense? It was hard to tell, but his expression remained neutral. Just a hint of anxiety in his eyes. "Thanks." I wouldn't make a deal out of this. I slipped the key into my jacket pocket before he decided to change his mind.

"And in case you still don't believe me…" He rose up on his toes and pushed his lips to mine. Very gently and without warning. A spark of electricity pulsed between us. I jerked back. Shocked at the suddenness, stunned by the pleasurable shivers tingling through every nerve ending. "I hope that makes up a bit for our spoiled afternoon."

Nothing was spoiled. I thought it had been, but this key, coupled with the kiss, meant every bit as much as the sex.

I stepped outside and caught a final smile before he closed the door.

# Chapter Twenty-One

"What's up?" Brian lowered his voice and leaned across the bar. "The fairy cakes gone stale already?"

I set the pint I'd just pulled down in front of him. "They're not fairy cakes. Don't call them that."

"Just a friendly euphemism." Brian gestured to his glass. "Got any nuts to go with this?"

I grabbed a pot from under the counter and slapped it down in front of him. Peanuts scattered across the bar, bouncing kamikaze-style into Brian's lap.

"Whoa!" Brain raised his palms. "I apologize for my choice of wording. You want me to go back to swingers?"

"How about you just don't mention them?"

"Why not? Oh yeah, I've asked that several times." When I didn't respond, Brian whistled out a breath. "Ah, mate. You fucked it all up, didn't you? No wonder you've been mooching about with a face like a boiled bollock. What'd you do this time?"

"Why does it have to be something I did?" I didn't blame myself. Not beyond wanting some quiet time with Piet. If I'd kept my mouth shut about seeing Nix while he and I were in the shower, then we could've had that perfect afternoon. Perfect until Piet found out about what Nix had seen and that I had seen Nix seeing what he'd seen. Then the shit would've hit the fan at an even greater rate than it already had. Not for the first time—actually more like the hundredth time—I had cause to wonder if I'd ever come out top in this relationship. In more ways than the obvious.

I left Brian playing with his nuts while I went to pour myself a coffee from the other end of the bar. It had been four days, and I'd heard nothing. Pieter hadn't called me or returned any of the voice mails I'd left.

"Just give me the bullet points," Brian said, when I returned from my coffee trip. "I've been married twenty years, so I know what goes in to making a successful relationship."

Brian might've been married twenty years, but he'd spent a month out of the last five at my place. Whenever he'd pissed his wife off so much she booted him out. Still, I had no one else to talk to. And I had zero experience in how to build a relationship that wasn't based on sex. *Considering sex is all Piet wanted from me, I really should be doing a hell of a lot better than this.*

"Piet said he'd call, and he hasn't." I heard the words repeated back at me in my head. I sounded like a teenaged girl who'd put out on the first date. "I don't know where I'm at. And he doesn't know what it is he wants."

Brian downed another mouthful of beer. "You haven't called them?"

Them. Not he. The plural jarred. It was never going to be just me and Piet, but whenever I thought of our 'relationship', it was me and it was him. Nix was the cantankerous in-law I had to keep on side if I wanted to make a go of things with Piet, even to the point of agreeing to this reckless bargain of his.

"I don't want to come across as desperate," I muttered, hoping he wouldn't catch the words.

Brian laughed. "You mean desperate as all those women whose calls you never return."

I clenched my fist in an effort to resist grabbing his glass and tipping the contents over his head. "I thought you were a self-confessed expert on dishing out relationship advice? You're doing a shit job of it so far."

"That's because I haven't started yet. Let me have a think." Brian picked up his pint and took a long draft. He savored the beer for several moments, then grabbed a handful of peanuts.

I waited patiently while he chomped through those. When he reached for another pawful, I swiped the bowl away. "I've called twice and left two voice mails. He hasn't got back to me. What does that say to you?"

"It says you're being blanked."

"But that doesn't even make sense." I'd raised my voice in my frustration, caught the attention of the few people still in the bar munching their way through their full English breakfasts. I lowered my voice. "The last time we were together, he gave me something. Something pretty intimate. So –"

"Fuck!" Brian pulled back. "Is it catching?"

I gave him an approximation of Nix's hard stare. "He gave me the key to his flat. Like as a symbol, to show how serious he is." It was also given as an apology for him kicking me out, but I'd take his explanation over my own slightly more cynical version.

"Phew. For a minute there I was worried." Brian hooked his elbows on the bar. "Have you tried using it, this key?"

"Nope." Piet had given me the thing, but it was like making an open dinner invitation to a vague acquaintance. You never plan for them to show up at your door, let alone let themselves in. "You think I should?"

"You want to find out one way or another if you've been dumped, go see the organ grinder. What's the worst that can happen?" The salacious smile returned. "With a bit of luck, you might end up getting your organ grinded."

I let Brian have his laugh, which lasted a good five seconds past what it should have. "You fancy taking over here for an hour or two? I'll pay you."

Brian's laughter dropped dead. "No chance. This is my day off. I'm only here for the staff discount on my beer."

I could persuade him. Brian had covered the bar before. Just not at such short notice. "How about free breakfasts for a week? On me."

"You'd have to double that to get a whisper of interest. Two weeks free lunches and I'll think about it. That's whatever I want off the menu, including a beer and pudding. Oh, and twice my hourly rate for however long I'm here. Plus, you have to be back before twelve. I'm not rushing myself into a heart attack once the lunchtime mob arrives."

I opened my mouth to tell him to fuck right off with that idea. But what other options were available? There was only me and one other behind the bar for another two hours. Couple that with the fact that I was on shift all day for the rest of the week and I still wasn't sure what nights Piet worked, either. I wanted to go see him while my mind was geared toward it.

"Deal. But I need to get changed first. Reckon you can start now?"

\* \* \* \*

Piet's car sat in its usual space outside his building, which meant the chances of him being home were good. I should have felt more relieved than I did.

But something must've happened that prevented him from contacting me. Selfish as it sounded, whatever it was wasn't going to be good for me. Or us. And I didn't want to use the key until I'd tested the water first.

So I played safe and pushed the intercom. Only when I didn't get a reply did I let myself in.

The air smelled different inside the flat. Usually the heat hit me walking through the door. Now the air weighed lighter, cooler. It was also utterly silent.

I headed down the hall and opened the lounge door. The curtains were still draped across the French doors, rendering the room dark as a cave. So it took me a moment to make out the figure hunched on the sofa with his knees drawn to his chest.

"Piet?"

The figure twitched. Piet raised his face. Too many shadows obscured his expression, but I could read the gloom on the air, see the huge glint of his eyes and the pale shard of a cheekbone.

I reached for the light and flicked it on.

"What do you want?" He didn't appear to be looking at me so much as straight through me.

"You didn't call. Or answer my calls." I swallowed down on the ominous sensation weighing heavy in my belly. "Where's Nix?"

"Why do you care? You haven't bothered to show your face in days."

"Have you been sitting here all this time waiting for my call?"

A flash of life finally lit his eyes. Eyes so dark they made his skin pale as Nix's. His freckled skin was sallow and clammy. A clear sheen glazed his forehead. "Why does everything have to be about you? You're such a vain, arrogant…annoyance."

*Vain and arrogant. True.* I'd been called far worse than an annoyance before. "If it's not to do with me, then why are you sitting here with the curtains pulled like a recently widowed vampire?"

"Because…" He drew another breath.

"What?" I swallowed. The ominous pit in my belly deepened. "Has something happened to Nix? Is he okay?" What if he wasn't? If he was in hospital. If Piet had been dealing with it all alone, thinking I didn't care enough even to…

"If you must know, he's left me."

My panic shut down. A slow numbness took over, made up mostly of confusion. Had I heard him wrong? Or was this part of some elaborate joke cooked up between them to punish me for welshing on Nix's bargain? But those weren't the types of games Piet played. This was serious. Real.

"Left you, how? He can hardly walk without help most of the time."

"You're concerned about how rather than why?" Piet tilted his head. "Do you think he's only physically left me? Cinder told me he's not sure he's ever coming back."

*Cinder? The mother.* Probably the woman responsible for this whole fucked-up marriage scenario in the first place. "Has he gone to stay with her?"

"He left a note on his pillow." Piet unfurled his legs.. "He seems to think you and me would do so much better without him getting in the way."

"Did he tell you that?"

He shook his head. "Cinder did, on his behalf. Over the phone. Do you have a cigarette?"

I reached into my jacket. Luckily for him, I'd bought a pack on my way here, to steady my nerves.

Piet snatched one from the offered pack. "And a light?"

"You're going to smoke in here?"

"Why not?" Piet plucked the lighter from my hand and sparked a flame. "Nix isn't here to stop me."

I took a cigarette for myself and joined him, though I felt uncomfortable enough to get up and open one of the French doors to the garden.

"Where's the note?" I asked, most of the way convinced he wasn't going to show it to me.

He paused long enough that I didn't think I was going to be wrong, then reached under a cushion and drew out a sheet of folded notepaper.

*Dear Piet*, was written at the top in a tiny, very neat scrawl. I could imagine Nix hunched over in bed, violet tresses falling on either side of his face as he pressed the black nib down on the sheet of plain, lineless paper.

*If you're wondering why I'm not at home, it's because I've left you. I've gone to stay with Cinder and Greg. I'm traveling by taxi and you don't have to worry about the bill because Greg is paying. Now you can spend time with Dean and I won't be in your way.*

*Love,*

*Phoenix Aaron Winterson-Croft*

"There aren't any kisses."

I looked up. "Huh?"

Piet tapped the note in my hand. "He always leaves an upside-down pyramid of kisses on his birthday and Christmas cards to me. Now he writes me a goodbye note, and there's nothing. See?" He pointed toward the empty space at the bottom of the page.

"It doesn't read like the kind of note that requires kisses," I said, with no hope of making him feel any better. "But he did put love here." I pointed at the word, as if he hadn't read this note a hundred times. The evidence was written in the crumpled paper and the dark circles beneath his eyes.

"He writes that to everyone, including emails to his hairdresser." Piet plucked the note from my hand. "He's only ever said he loves me once in his life and I had to prompt him into saying it."

"He said it to me." When Piet look up from the note, with horror etched across his face, I quickly added, "About you, I mean. He said he loved you."

"When?"

"That day he was ill." I stubbed my cigarette out in the ashtray between us. "He said you were his, and that you'd never leave him."

"So he leaves me instead?" Piet ground out his cigarette in the ashtray. "Let him see his mistake when Cinder doesn't have the time to take care of him properly." The bitterness suggested he was speaking from prior experience.

179

"You know there's nothing wrong with making the first move." I may have had my doubts about their relationship, but they evidently needed each other. There wasn't much passion — actually, no passion — but that didn't make them any less real. "There's no way you're going to be any good to anyone without him."

Piet tugged the note away from me and carefully refolded it. "Haven't I told you to go?"

"No. But you throw me out if you like. That's the only way I'm leaving." I rose from the sofa and headed for the kitchen. "How about I make us a coffee while you go shower?"

"What makes you think I won't throw you out?"

"Not counting me being taller and heavier than you?"

"If I wanted to, I could." His sinister undertones sparked the most inconvenient heat in my cock. "Just because he's gone, it doesn't mean you get to take his place."

I paused, halfway to opening a cupboard. "I don't want to take his place."

"Then what do you want?"

"For now? Making plans to get Nix back where he belongs. Which is here. With you." When I turned around, he was standing directly behind me in his shorts and a thin T-shirt. His face looked like he didn't know what day it was, just that it was a day he would rather have spent in hibernation.

"I lost my job," he said. Half-blurted, really.

"And that's my fault?" I thought I'd say it before he got there, as if that would make the accusation less painful. It was something we were both thinking — had to be.

Piet shook his head. "No. It's my fault. I like you more than the little bit we agreed. I have for a while. I ignored it because I'm selfish. Now I've lost Phoenix. I've lost everything."

"You haven't lost him. We're going to get him back."

"Are we?" He didn't sound convinced. I, on the other hand, didn't have a single doubt.

"Yep. Now let me get on with making this coffee." I took out the jar of instant, knowing he still stood there watching my every move. I thought if I tried to keep on the level, then he would, too. He was a freak-out waiting to happen – the air was charged with his grief and his rage at himself. For thinking that his was all him. When in fact, half of it was me. And part of it was Nix. We were all to blame, although I didn't think it would be a good idea to say so right now.

When a knock sounded at the door, I almost dropped a mug.

"You going to get that?" I asked. As far as I was concerned, there was only one person on the other side of the door. Although Nix would have used his key.

"No. I'm going for the shower you told me to have."

"But it could be Nix."

Piet paused in the doorway. "It isn't."

"Who else would it be?"

"Cinder. She said she was on her way. Answer it, if you must. Personally, I wouldn't bother." With that he disappeared. Next thing I heard was the bathroom door shut.

# Chapter Twenty-Two

I'd imagined Phoenix's mother as some hippy-dippy flake of a middle-aged woman. Long unkempt hair streaked with silver, tambourine for a handbag.

The woman on the other side of the door was nothing like the woman I'd pictured. For starters, she wasn't all done up in some floaty floral ensemble made up of charity shop curtains. She wore a fitted black velvet jacket and a pair of jeans that showed off a fine if skinny figure. Her short hair was dark, her face sharp.

"Dean, I presume." She sounded like she'd caught me cleaning the toilet with my tongue.

"That's me."

"Is Pieter in?" She tried to peer past me. Even in those spiky-heeled ankle boots, she was no taller than my shoulder. "Or has he taken to hiding?"

"He's in the shower."

"Really?" She didn't sound too convinced. "I'm Phoenix's mother. I assume I am permitted inside?"

Like I had any authority to tell her she wasn't.

I stepped back.

As she passed me, a waft of sickly perfume swept up my nostrils. I sneezed and shut the door.

If she had any doubts as to Piet's whereabouts, the sound of water thrashing down on the shower cubicle beyond the bathroom door proved my sincerity. She glanced at the door before carrying on down to the lounge.

"You want a tea or something while you're waiting?"

"Peppermint, if you have it." She perched on the edge of the armchair. "Or rather, if Pieter has it, since this isn't your home."

*Ouch.* I wouldn't rise to it. I had an inkling of what she must think about me if Nix had been filling her in.

I rooted through the kitchen cupboards, feeling her scan my every move from the armchair.

"Is he okay?" I asked, when the silence itched every bit as much as her attention. "Phoenix, I mean."

"Not remotely." Her clipped tones left me in no doubt that I was the bad guy. "Please don't feign concern on my account. I'm aware of the part you've played in this fiasco."

I busied myself juggling a freshly boiled kettle, a tea bag, three mugs and the coffee jar. "I won't deny I played a part in him leaving, but it was all down to a misunderstanding." I took the milk from the fridge. "How do you take it?"

"Take what?"

"Your tea. Milk, sugar?"

"In peppermint tea?"

She sounded like I'd offered to load her cup up with Tabasco sauce. Which, come to think of it, Piet did have some of at the back of the cupboard. I almost made to reach for it, but Piet was clearly in enough trouble with her as it was.

"Tell me," she said as I set her tea down on the side table. "What does someone like you see in a boy like Pieter?" Her gaze dropped to my chest, then past my abs to my fly. "I find your interest quite…bewildering."

"There's plenty to see." I let the double meaning carry, refusing to let her intimidate me. "Like, all the things your son sees."

"Until you came along." She daintily gripped the cup's handle and lifted. "Then those things were no longer good enough." She took a sip of tea. The resulting wince mimicked her son's exactly. It wasn't as if anyone could go wrong shoving a fucking tea bag in a cup of hot water.

"It wasn't your fault."

I looked to where the voice had come from.

Piet stood in the doorway, dressed in jeans and a sweatshirt. His damp hair stuck up in spikes, but he smelled sweeter than he had earlier. His glasses were firmly in place, too. I didn't blame him for wanting to hide behind them. I bet Cinder could be a scary bitch when she got going.

I fought the urge to take his hand. Now wasn't the time to give Cinder any detail of our feelings. Or my feelings. I wasn't even sure what Piet's were, if anything, for me.

"Nix and I were in trouble long before you showed up."

His words should have rested more easily with me than they did, but there was no getting away from the fact that Nix had left because of me.

"Whatever your problems, Pieter," Cinder said, casting the illusion of calm despite the clenched hands in her lap, "I daresay my son walking in on his husband

and his lover rutting in the shower didn't serve your marriage any favors, either."

A stiff silence settled over us. I took a seat next to Piet on the sofa. His face had turned the color of the magnolia walls and I could feel my own flaming like the gates of hell. I could imagine the exacting details Nix would have felt the need to go into while he was telling that particular story.

"Nix said he was fine about Dean," Piet said softly, almost as if he were taking to himself. "He always has been about the others. I—"

"Others?" Cinder banged her tea down on the side table without spilling a drop. "You bring home men to screw right under his nose, knowing how ill he is?" Some of her hard face cracked. Her glossy pink lips trembled. I had a vision of her disintegrating in a flood of tears.

Piet's expression remained tough as a shield. "Don't act so shocked. When you and my mother were together, there were often new faces at the breakfast table."

"That was completely different and you—"

"Wait a minute." I put up my hand. This was something I needed to hear repeated. "Your mums were doing each other? Like, lesbians?"

"Well done, Dean. You're quite the label queen." Cinder slow-clapped twice. "Funny, but you give nothing away in your sense of…" She looked me up and down, and not for the first time. "…style."

I'd assumed that Piet's mum had paired up with Nix's dad. Not that it made a difference. It was slack of me to presume a hetero relationship. "I'm no queen," I muttered. It hardly needed saying. She could see that clearly for herself.

"Dean's bisexual and proud." Piet grabbed a coffee from the table and took a long sip. "I'm gay, and I don't mind about the label." He placed the mug back down and slipped his hand into my jacket pocket. He brought out my pack of cigarettes. "Nix is asexual but doesn't want to admit it." He took out a cigarette. "And I can't be celibate. I've tried. It's impossible." When he lit the cigarette, his hand trembled only slightly. The no smoking in the house rule had well and truly been blown out of the window. Phoenix, being asexual, hadn't blown anything. And wasn't ever likely to.

Cinder opened her mouth. No words came out. She tried again. "Are you trying to tell me you and Phoenix haven't…"

"Yes. I mean, we have. Of course. Just, not for a long time." Pieter took a deep draw on the cigarette. "We have our arrangement. Nix has never had a problem with it before."

Cinder gestured to Piet's cigarette. "I'll take one of those, if you don't mind."

*Everyone's a smoker.* I got up and handed Cinder the pack, followed by a light. She settled back in the chair, a puff of smoke breezing from between her lips. "So Phoenix did agree to this?"

"It was his idea," Piet said, way more calmly than I was feeling. "I mean, about asking Dean to stay. He made the invitation."

She said something else, but I was distracted by my phone vibrating in my pocket. I pulled it out and checked the screen. Brian. I'd forgotten about him valiantly covering for me back at work.

*Where r u? Getting busy here. R not happy.*

R being the bar manager, who was never happy anyway. Least of all with me. Work was the last thing on my mind, and for what Brian was getting in return compensation-wise, he could stay a little longer.

I thumbed back a quick message — *Soz busy myself. Call u l8r* — then switched my phone off before sliding it back into my jeans' pocket.

"Well?"

I looked up.

Cinder was staring at me. She'd obviously asked something and was expecting an answer. Had she just asked who I was texting? Despite the fact it had zero to do with her.

"Uh, just a mate. From work."

"What was?"

"The text." When I looked at Piet, his expression was no more clued in than Cinder's. "I mean, it wasn't Nix. I don't think he even has my number."

Piet released a heavy breath. "Cinder asked what your stake in our relationship was."

"Did she?" There was an innuendo waiting to be revealed, but it wasn't in my interest to reveal it. I cleared my throat instead. "I guess it's more than just the obvious. I mean, sex." I was aware of Piet next to me, squirming a hole into the sofa cushion. "I like hanging out with both of them. Piet and Nix. I enjoy their company. They make me feel like I'm —"

"Wait." Piet touched my arm. "You enjoy Nix's company?"

"Yeah. Or I wouldn't have said so." I didn't see why this should prove to be such a revelation. I must've enjoyed Nix's company or I would have given up on Piet as soon as I'd found out about him. "I find him strangely entertaining." And visually hypnotic, but that was all to do with sexual attraction. A subject best avoided when it came to my feelings for Nix. "I like him. I like the two of you. I like us."

Piet stubbed his cigarette out next to mine in the ashtray. "Can we come back with you?" He aimed the question at Cinder, who was listening to our conversation with a neutrality she hadn't shown before. "We need to see him."

"We?" Cinder glanced my way. "You want to bring him?"

"There's a few things I'd like to say to Phoenix," I said. I'd been partway responsible for him leaving and I needed him to know I wasn't a threat. "If it helps get him home, I'd appreciate the opportunity to say them."

# Chapter Twenty-Three

When we pulled up in front of a large Victorian terrace in the heart of SW-10, I had to reevaluate my thoughts on Nix's family home, just like I had with his mother. *No hippy-dippy rambling country house, this.*

Black railings lined the front wall and window boxes bloomed with brightly colored flowers. I wondered where her cannabis farm bloomed. *Probably in the basement. I bet she has a whole business down there, supplying half the street.* Nix would deny it if asked.

I had to wonder how a mother living in Chelsea seemed perfectly happy to see her disabled son and his husband renting a rabbit-hutch flat off the council.

"She married into it," Piet said, as though he was actually reading my thoughts. We were sitting in Cinder's Range Rover, waiting for her to prep Phoenix for our arrival. "Her current husband's a business analyst."

"Current? How many has she had?"

"A few. They're all rebounds."

"From who? Your mum?"

"No." Piet snorted. "That was never anything serious. She's only ever really been in love with Nix's dad."

"And where's he?"

"He left her after she had Nix. According to Cinder, he preferred fucking around like an irresponsible teenager to taking responsibility for his family." Piet cast a sidelong look at me. "I've seen photos. He was very good-looking."

"I hope you're not about to accuse me of wanting to shag a bloke I've never even met."

"Of course not. Besides which, he looks a lot like Phoenix." Piet went back to watching the traffic pass by out of the window. "So you'd claim not to be interested, anyway."

I opened the car door.

"Where are you going?"

I nodded toward the house. Cinder was on the doorstep, beckoning us in. I didn't want to get into another argument about not having sex with someone I was pretty sure didn't want to have sex with me anyway.

The front door opened onto a wide, wooden-floored hallway. There was a set of stairs to my right, and to the left a set of double doors opened onto a sizable dining room.

"He's out on the terrace," she said. "Greg set him up with a laptop and a flask of tea before he had to leave for work. Will you be staying the night?"

"I don't know. It depends on how things go." Piet glanced at me, like I was expected to help him out. But clearly that overnight invitation didn't include me. I'd be expected to get the train home.

"I'll need to get something in for dinner, either way." She slipped past me, to the door. "I'll take my time so you can have a proper discussion." She made a point of looking at me. "I hope you were honest earlier about helping them. They need each other. I daresay a lot more than they need you."

"Dean knows that," Piet said, rather helpfully cementing my lack of importance. Although, I would step aside if my being here was worse than my not being here. Fixing them, like they wanted me to, was going to take a lot more than getting Nix to agree to come home.

*One step at a time.*

Cinder slipped out of the door then, leaving us alone in the house. Except for Nix on the top floor.

"Is that for Nix?" I gestured to a stairlift as we took the first flight.

"Yes. The previous owners left it. Just as well, seeing as our room's right at the top of the house."

"Your own room?" I didn't know why I sounded so impressed. I suppose this meant they weren't as isolated as I'd assumed them to be.

"We also have a room at my mum's. Don't you at yours?"

I had no fuckin' clue. Any room that I may have had once had probably been converted into a home gym by now. "I don't see them that much."

"That's sad." When I caught a glimpse of his face, he didn't look as though he meant sad as in pathetic. More sad as in…sad.

"This house is nice," I said, awkwardly moving the conversation on. The house, rather than my parents' sprawling but ultimately soulless ranch-style abode in the middle of the Sussex countryside, had a soul. A scent of lavender and ectoplasm from the ghosts of all the people who'd lived and died in these walls.

"It's nothing like the place Nix and I grew up in," Piet said with a wistful sigh. "That house was only held up by cobwebs and dust."

No dust here. Not a speck that I could see. They probably had a cleaner. Or employed Piet to clean when he came to visit.

"You'll have to tell me about it sometime."

"You genuinely want to know, or are you just interested in the lesbian mums thing?"

Fuck he was making me sound perverted. Like Brian, who most definitely would be interested in the lesbian mums thing. "I was just surprised about that. Not obsessed."

"Good. Because if you ever get to meet my mum, you should know she's still a lesbian. And I'd hate for that to be a thing for you."

"It wouldn't be." I joined him on the landing. "You want me to meet your mum?"

"I said if, didn't I?"

"You wouldn't be saying that if you were going to sack me off."

"It's not up to me," he said with a rather camp toss of his head. "It depends what Phoenix wants."

The attic room was a surprisingly airy space with a double bed at one end, and a set of double doors led out onto a wooden terrace on the other. The terrace was furnished by a couple of wrought iron chairs and a table.

Nix was out there in his pajamas, bundled up in several blankets. He had a laptop, a bowl of cherries and a flask on a tray. No wonder he'd chosen to come here. He had everything on tap.

Piet went outside while I hung back in the doorway. They needed to talk to each other, and anything I might want to say could wait.

"You could have phoned." Nix glanced up from the laptop. "If you absolutely must talk, don't take long. I'm very busy."

"Busy doing what?"

"Researching divorce," Nix announced, obviously taking pride in his forward thinking. "The first thing we need to do is appoint a solicitor. Each. We can't have the same one. It says here that would be a..." He squinted at the screen. "Conflict of interests."

"We don't need solicitors, Phoenix."

"Oh? Do you think we could do it ourselves?" He scratched at his bobble hat. "I suppose it would save money."

"No, I mean we can't get divorced. I won't agree to it. So you can close that laptop."

Nix cast a sly glance my way, then leaned across the table. "But what about Dean?" He dropped his voice to a stage whisper. "Won't you want to marry him instead? It's illegal to have two husbands. Even if we get a religion. I've checked online."

Piet turned to me and rolled his eyes. "This is the main reason we don't have the internet at home."

Since Piet appeared to want me to be a part of the conversation, I stepped outside, too. If this was all about humoring Phoenix until his senses returned, that was the least I owed.

I approached the table, though there wasn't anywhere for me to sit so I loitered. "I can't marry Piet, anyway."

"Why not?"

"Because it's not me he loves."

"You mean, there's someone else?" Nix's gaze snapped to Piet. "Who?"

Piet shook his head. He seemed calm, considering. "No. It's just you. Always."

"I've seen you two together." Nix closed the laptop. "I can't like sex the way you do. Not even with Dean."

I wanted to tell him I could hear every word, but if he thought I remained oblivious to what he was stage-whispering, then who was I to destroy his illusion?

There was an ensuite to my left, the door having been left open. "Can I use the loo?"

"Of course. If you need to, you must go." Nix looked down his nose at me. "We both know what happens when a bladder is left too long."

I nipped into the bathroom sharpish, before Piet asked him to elaborate. Nix could divulge the details of that particular incident himself.

I sat on the side of the bath and switched my phone on.

I had a bunch of texts from Brian, becoming increasingly urgent and more abusive and culminating in a final two-word sign-off that had been sent just over an hour before.

*U Cunt*

I sent him a quick text back.

*£350 + all meals for a month.*

My entire week's wage, because I didn't get an enhanced salary like most of the staff seemed to assume I did. And I didn't want to piss Brian off. It wasn't like I could afford to lose the few mates I did have.

He responded a minute or so later.

*Deal. (still a cunt)*

I could live with that.

I sat on the loo and stared at the door, determined not to listen in. This conversation wasn't for my ears.

I lit up a cigarette and blew the smoke at the extractor fan until there was a polite knock on the door. I dropped the filter down the toilet, then sprayed around a bit of air freshener that I'd found on a shelf.

"Dean?"

I opened the door.

Piet was waiting for me, looking grim but not devastated. "Nix wants us all to talk."

*Now that doesn't sound ominous. Much.*

I shut the door behind me.

Nix was inside now, seated on the bed, minus his blankets and hat. His violet hair stuck up in all directions and his lips were still faintly stained with cherry juice. "You can't not see him anymore. Piet wouldn't like that."

"I don't want to not see him," I said, wary of just how volatile this situation could potentially become. "But you and Piet need to sort yourselves out first, before you start worrying about me."

"Does that mean you are dumping him? To have sex with someone else?"

I looked at Piet, seeking assistance. He lifted a shoulder. *No help at all.*

I took a seat next to him on the bed and touched the voluminous pajama sleeve engulfing his arm. "I don't want sex with anyone else. The two of you are more than enough for me."

Nix twitched inside the sleeve. "It's not me. It's just Piet."

"I don't think he means it like that," Piet said, finding his voice.

"I don't."

Nix stared up at me, with the same impassive expression that seemed to be his default. Wanting me to elaborate.

"What I mean is that it needs to be you and Piet. So that you can decide between yourselves if there's going to be space for me."

"That's no good." Nix knocked my hand away. "Who's he supposed to get sex from in the meantime?"

"For gods' sakes, Phoenix." Piet cringed in his shoes. "I can go without."

"No, you can't. All you'll do is go back to playing with those toys you have and masturbating all over the sheets."

"*Phoenix.*"

I felt his embarrassment, hot as all those sheets he must've come over.

I turned around. Piet was practically melting. "Toys?"

"That's private," he muttered, mid-squirm.

"He has a collection of penises," Phoenix announced with a pride that should have been reserved for war medals.

"It's not a collection," Piet was quick to say, still with his head down. No way could he blame his pink face on the weak sunlight filtering through the clouds.

"He has ten of them. All different shapes and sizes and colors. Some of them vibrate. That's a collection."

"You got ten dildos?" Their flat was a shoebox. "Where do you put them all?"

196

"Where do you think?" Nix piped up. "He put them all up his —"

"The wardrobe," Piet blurted, raising his voice to carry above Nix's. "In a couple of boxes. They were presents. Which is another reason we no longer have a computer. Now can we please not talk about them anymore?"

For a minute, we could. But later, if there was to be a later for us, I'd want details. And full visual proof that he did indeed own ten dildos of assorted colors. Some of which vibrated. Those ones especially warranted further investigation.

"You don't kiss me."

Both Piet and I shifted our attention to Nix.

"Why would you say that?" Piet said briskly. "I kiss you all the time."

"The last time you kissed me properly was fourteen months ago. It was also the last time you ejaculated in my mouth."

"Oh. God." Piet crashed both hands through his hair. "We really need this discussion in private."

Nix, who I doubted had ever experienced a shade of embarrassment in all his life, not counting the naked phobia, stood his ground. "You don't ask me to do that for you anymore."

"You know why that is." Piet's shoulders dropped. I wanted to place my supportive hands on them, but the move would be a bad one, so I refrained. "Because you want someone pretty, like Dean. Someone who can do all the things that he does and better than I can do it. There's something wrong with me, and I don't think I can be fixed."

"There's nothing wrong with you," I said, although I'd told him this before and it hadn't sunk it then, either.

"Just like there's nothing wrong with Piet or with me. We just enjoy different things."

"I don't. I don't enjoy any of it."

"You enjoy kissing."

"Yes. But only that."

"There's stuff I don't like with sex," I said, racking my brains to think of something.

"I know. Like having Piet's penis in your anus. You said you wouldn't like that."

Piet let out a choked breath. "When did you discuss this?"

"Doesn't matter." I needn't have bothered to think quite so hard to come up with something when Nix could take care of it in an instant. "But, yeah. That's something neither me or Piet would want."

"Who says I wouldn't?"

"Are you telling me I'm wrong?"

"No. But you can't just assume."

"He can," Nix said, back to his usual hyper-volume. "Just like you do. All the time."

"I don't."

"You assume I don't want you kissing me. And that I don't want to help you ejaculate." Annoyance sparked off his gaze. "Both of you assume I don't want to be a part of you. That I'm to be separate. That I have to go to bed alone. It's not what I want."

"It isn't?" Piet and I both spoke at the same time, then looked at each other.

"No."

"What are you saying?" Piet asked, his voice thin with hesitation.

"I could hazard a guess at what he's saying." Unlike Piet, I couldn't pretend I didn't know exactly what was running through Nix's mind.

# Chapter Twenty-Four

"You tell him," Nix said.

I shook my head. "Nah. You'll put it so much more eloquently than me."

Piet eyed me first, then Nix. "Tell me what?

Nix poked me in the biceps. "You're wearing too many clothes."

I gestured to Piet. "I'll strip when he does."

Piet wrapped both arms around himself. "I'm not taking my clothes off."

That sounded like something Nix would say, minus the conviction. Piet knew exactly what we had in mind.

"Piet." Nix sounded almost gentle in his coaxing, which had to be a first for him. "I don't have enough energy to play this game."

"What game?"

"The game where you pretend you don't want something to happen when really you do." Nix turned to me. "Have you got any condoms?"

The subject change caught me off guard. I fumbled for my wallet and brought out the two I had, then held them up like prizes.

Piet stared at us both in turn, a stunned horror that no one should be wearing for an invitation to a three-way fixed on his face.

"This is ridiculous. Phoenix, you don't like sex. You never have."

"There are things I can do." Nix plucked the condom from my raised hand. "Dean can take care of everything else."

"What about lube?" I asked, knowing I'd potentially spoiled the moment. We'd done it without in the shower, but I didn't fancy trying the same thing now. This was going to be tricky enough.

"Piet." Nix flapped a hand at the door. "Fetch one of Cinder's massage oils. The one that doesn't smell."

Piet lifted his chin. "He wants it, he can get it."

He being me, presumably.

"It's not for him." Nix placed the condoms very carefully on the bedside table. "It's for you."

They stared each other out, raising the temperature of the room several degrees. Then Piet's jaw unlocked. He strode across the room, pulled open the door and slammed it shut behind him.

"You think we went a little too far?" I asked, because I don't think either of us had considered the possibility Piet wasn't going to come back.

"No." Nix toed off his shoes and put his feet up on the mattress. "Sit with me."

"Are you sure about this?" I asked, for what felt like the hundredth time. "Piet told me you weren't exactly impressed by what you saw the other afternoon."

"I'm not participating in anything like that." His shudder vibrated through the mattress. "No one is putting their penis in me."

"Wouldn't dream of it." I drew the blinds across the glass doors, took off my shoes and joined him on the bed.

Nix flipped on the bedside table lamp. "I don't mind helping you enjoy sex. Or Piet. But I don't understand why you like it so much." He shifted a little closer to me. "I find it—"

"Horrific, according to Piet."

"Horrendous, actually." Nix nodded a little more forcefully than was warranted. "I never thought that it would be so violent."

"Hey, come on. It was nothing like violent."

"It was. Piet never did it to me like that, and there isn't anyone in the world who could teach me to want that done to me."

Time to lighten the mood. "You ever thought you might be straight?"

His eyes widened. "You mean heterosexual?"

No, I'd meant it as a joke, not something for deep consideration. His tone suggested he thought otherwise, so I decided to carry the idea a little further. "Do you fancy women?"

"Like who?"

"I don't know. Any of the women you know. Do you get excited at the thought of taking them to bed?"

A little curl tugged at the corner of his mouth. "Do you mean like Anita?"

"I don't know who Anita is, but is she attractive?"

"I don't think so. Not like you are."

"Okay. Well. That makes you at least bi…"

The door opened. Piet returned. He stopped. Looked at me, then at Nix. "What were you talking about?"

"Dean thinks I should have sex with Anita," Nix said, blunt as ever. "To see if I'm heterosexual like she is."

I gritted my teeth. "That is not what I said."

"He's not heterosexual." Piet set a small bottle of oil down next to the condoms on my side of the bed. "And he doesn't need to sleep with his step-sister to know it."

*Step-sister. Fuck.* Nix might've released that little nugget of information before I'd just made a total tit of myself. I nudged his shoulder. "Thanks for making me out as the pervert."

"You hardly need any help there." Piet perched on the end of the mattress and took off his shoes. "We're only doing this because Nix thinks it's good idea. Let's be clear on that."

"Naturally." I patted the narrow strip of mattress between me and Nix. "We saved a space for your reluctant arse right here."

"Fuck you."

"Nope, that's your privilege." I had the good grace to keep any rogue laughter off my face, but I was tiring of his faux reluctance. "Look. Since you haven't run off, we know you're going to give this a go. You might even end up having fun."

Piet crossed his arms. "I'm only staying because Phoenix insisted."

"Whatever your reasons." I again patted the mattress and shifted closer to him. "You going to join us or are we heading down there to join you?"

Piet stared at my hand. At first, I thought I'd pushed too far and he'd storm away. But no. He climbed into the vacant space between Nix and me.

He sat back against the headboard, hands in his lap, and waited. His breath came in short hitches, his nerves betraying him.

"Hey." I slipped a hand across his thigh. "If you don't want this, we call it off. We can all agree on that, can't we?"

"Yes," Nix said, though I hadn't been talking to him. He straddled Piet's thighs the way he'd straddled mine not so long ago. "This will be good for all of us." He clasped Piet's sweatshirt in both fists then leaned in. Their lips touched, very tentatively, then Nix pulled back.

"That's how you kiss me. Now I'm going to show you how I kiss Dean," he said. All of a sudden, he was our hands-on tutor in all things erotic.

I braced for Piet to knock that idea on the head.

"Okay," he said.

"Good." Nix let go of him and bunched a fist in my T-shirt. He yanked me close with a strength I never would have attributed to him, even on a good day.

His open lips crushed against mine. His tongue thrust into my mouth, pulsing with desire, as if he'd been saving it all up from all those frustrating months when Piet had withdrawn from any hint of passion and now he was spending it all on me.

But Piet was under him, as I was hotly aware. Our mouths clashed. I tasted cherries sweet as my arousal, yet none of this was going any further. None of this was about me.

Nix broke the kiss, then turned to Piet. "That was how you used to kiss me. Before you stopped."

It was a shame Nix wasn't into fucking. The things I could imagine me and Piet doing to him to wring out his pleasure. Make him like it, except I had a feeling we could no more make Nix like sex than we could make Piet straight. Or me choose which sex I preferred.

"I didn't think you—"

Nix dived at him and pushed his lips over Piet's still-talking mouth. A delicious attack that spoke of want and need and the fire of a passion that could never spark a flame. Not for him. It was totally different for those he shared his kisses with. Now it was my turn to watch and appreciate. Because I did appreciate the sight of two twinks getting it on.

Their lips melded together. Nix still clung to the front of Piet's sweatshirt, and Piet had shifted his hands to Nix's cheeks, holding him while their wet mouths accommodated their equally hot tongues.

A low growl rumbled at the back of Piet's throat. He'd made that sound before, with me. The sound of his desire, however stifled. He could find release with Nix, yet I was hoping he'd need me somewhere along the line.

Nix didn't break their kiss as he had with me. When it drew to a natural conclusion, they both parted. A thin string of saliva connected their lips.

"Do you remember when it used to be like that?" Nix asked, his voice thin.

"Of course I do." Piet's lashes lowered. When he raised them, a tear slipped down his cheek. "I'm sorry."

"Doesn't matter." Nix unlatched his fist from Piet's clothing. "Now you have to kiss Dean."

Piet's head shot up. "What?"

"I've kissed him. Quite a bit."

"But that was just a one-off. And it should never have happened. You—"

"No, it wasn't. We kissed just the other day. In the shower."

This kid really did have a gob the size of my libido.

Piet's fiery gaze locked on me. His left eyelid twitched. "In. The. Shower?"

"He also saw me naked," Nix piped up, like he hadn't just derailed any prospect of this three-way or whatever the hell it was going to be. "But that doesn't matter now we're all in bed together. You should kiss him before he decides he'd rather kiss me again instead."

Piet blinked. The rage burning up his pupils flickered out. "Would you?"

Loaded question. A yes would get me into the piss with Piet. A no and I'd be treated to Nix's icy tongue. "I've been wanting to kiss you since we met."

"Why?"

I wasn't trying to trick him into anything. He knew how much I wanted his lips on mine. There was no need to play this game.

"Because I like to kiss just as much as your husband does. Any issue with that seems to be with you rather than us."

"It's not an issue. It's…"

"Yes?" I leaned slightly closer. His breath was hot with all those unspoken word he couldn't seem to bring himself to say.

Nix gave him a nudge. "He'll never be less submissive if you don't make him take charge." He dropped his voice to his usual stage-whisper. "When I want him to kiss me, I have to make the first move. He's too shy to do it himself."

We were back to that shy thing again? I'd thought I'd dispelled that particular misconception. *Evidently not.* "If I thought he wanted me to kiss him, I would have by now. Like I told you before, I don't force myself on anyone."

"You should." Nix climbed off Piet's thighs and pushed himself back against the pillows. "That's how he likes it."

"No, it isn't." Piet turned to me. "Nix doesn't know anything."

"I do," Nix said, practically invisible now he'd settled behind Piet. "I know you want to kiss Dean."

"I know you want to kiss him more," Piet shot back over his shoulder. Then he jabbed me in the chest. "And you don't need to look so smug about it, either."

What was there to be smug about, listening to the two of them bickering over who wanted to snog me more? "I'm just waiting for the two of you to come to a decision."

"If you don't want a kiss, I'll take one." Nix half-climbed, half-lurched across his husband, one knee poised dangerously close to Piet's groin.

"Wait." Piet pushed a hand to his chest. "I didn't say I wouldn't."

"Then don't make so much fuss. Dean's kisses are very warm. You'd like them."

"Maybe I would. It's just…" Piet glanced at me, then pushed his mouth to Nix's ear. "I've never kissed anyone else before."

"That's all right." Nix's face brightened. "Dean's kissed hundreds of boys. He's very experienced."

I cleared my throat. "I wouldn't say hundreds." Not if it were just boys. "But I've never had any complaints."

"Good. Piet will take one." Nix gave him a little shove toward me. "Hurry up before he changes his mind."

*Absolutely no chance of that.*

Piet sucked in a shuddering breath, then straddled my thighs. "I think you should know that I'm doing this for Nix, not for you."

"Yeah, you've made that clear."

He narrowed his eyes again. "Why are you being like this?"

"Like what?"

"Passive."

"Is that not how you want me to be?"

"Definitely not," Nix said with far too much gravitas.

"Okay."

"What does that—?"

I grabbed Piet. Couldn't help myself. I yanked him forward. Ours lips collided. His mouth was open, though stiff. I teased my tongue in there, just the tip in case he flirted with any notion of biting down. But no teeth were forthcoming. Instead his lips relaxed around mine, then ripened into action.

His tongue met mine with an enthusiastic flick. I almost pulled back, because I'd expected a battle. He'd hardly given a hint he'd wanted this. Yet his mouth was electric, sparking straight to my cock. His tongue returned, full force this time, raking over my teeth.

I released my grip on his arms, slipped them around his waist and hooked my fingers under his T-shirt to feel the heat of his skin.

From somewhere close, I heard a voice. I couldn't make out the words and didn't want to. So I ignored it and instead chose to lose myself in the sweet flavors of his mouth.

The voice sounded again. Something hard and bony bit into my arm.

"I said that's enough."

The same hard boniness transferred from my arm to my shoulder. Piet's lips were wrenched from mine.

I opened my eyes. Piet was staring at me, glassy-eyed and panting. His mouth was pink and bruised. I daresay my own sported a similar hue.

"It was supposed to be one kiss." Nix shoved himself between us, one hand on my shoulder, the other on Piet's chest. "This is about me, too. Or had you forgotten?"

"It was just the one kiss, Phoenix," Piet said quietly.

"Yes, but it lasted four times as long as a normal kiss." He glanced at me, then returned his attention to Piet. "You're wearing too many clothes. Dean and I need to help you out of them."

# Chapter Twenty-Five

"Why do I have to take off my clothes first?" Piet turned his sulk on me. "It should be Dean."

"It's you because I'm in charge." Nix half-tugged, half-yanked Piet off my lap. "Lift your arms."

Piet's lips tightened. Rather than whine about his situation, he actually did as he'd been told.

Nix brought the sweatshirt up over his head, then threw it to one side. "Dean, take off his jeans and his underwear."

I had nothing to whine about, either. I rose from the bed and went to stand at the end.

Piet's feet retreated up the mattress. "I can do that myself."

"No, you can't." Nix popped the button on Piet's jeans. "And anyway, you're not getting a say."

I waited until Piet gave in and pushed his feet back toward me. Then I caught the heel in my palm and eased the sock away. The sole of his foot was slightly roughened, like his hands.

I'd never taken the time to appreciate the unwrapping of a person before. Their clothing was usually nothing more than a hindrance, an unwanted delay before pushing up inside them en route to gratification.

I removed his other sock, then tugged at his jeans. He even lifted his backside without being told. He sported pink pants this time, emblazoned with yet another familiar character. A budding erection made Animal's face bulge.

I ran my tongue around my dry lips. "You look so pretty."

"Don't tell him." Nix rested his hand on Piet's belly. "You'll make him vain."

I didn't think vanity would ever be an issue with Piet. Nix, on the other hand, wore his with pride. The evidence lie in his eccentric choice of clothing, coupled with a vast array of products with which to treat his violet hair.

"What about his underwear?" Nix rubbed a thumb an inch below the waistband of Piet's pants. "These need to go, too."

I met Piet's gaze. "That okay with you?"

"Does my opinion matter?"

His opinion mattered most of all, but, if I said as much, the illusion would shatter. Piet hadn't been forced into this, but maybe he was trying to convince himself he had been.

"Nope." I grasped his pants either side of his hips and yanked them to his thighs. His cock sprang free, full and thickening. As curious as I was to taste, I held off. He'd always been touchy about me not going there with my mouth. But I paused long enough to let him know how tempted I was.

Piet's legs twitched. I looked up to find his eyes closed, chin raised, riding the pleasure pounding through his hard cock.

Nix tugged my arm. "Now you."

I tossed Piet's pants to the floor. "Now me, what?"

"You have to take off your clothes."

Piet opened his eyes and met my gaze.

I didn't need telling twice.

I tore off my stuff and left everything on the floor where it fell. I stood before them, naked, my cock posturing under their gazes.

I tossed the bottle of oil into Nix's lap. "Do you know how to get him ready for me?"

"Yes. I've done it before. When he used the toys."

"Oh, we're definitely going to give that some further exploration when we get back."

In the meantime, Piet's shaft stood proud, a brooding shade of rose against his pale belly He slipped down on the mattress and lifted his knees to his chest without being asked. Or told.

"I appreciate your compliance." As I strolled to the foot of the bed, I also appreciated the view. I'd never seen him from this angle before. "Your enthusiasm."

"He's always been enthusiastic when it comes to sex," Nix supplied, with his usual prideful boast.

"Phoenix," Piet hissed.

"Weren't you told not to speak?" I knelt on the bottom of the bed. "Part your knees." My breathiness surprised me. But it wasn't like I could hide what I was feeling. My cock was hot and flush, desperate for attention.

Piet's expression remained tense, but his knees eased away from each other until he was as open to me as he'd ever been. His piquant scent clouded my thoughts, and I wanted to do nothing more than sink into him, naked and raw, and make him cry my name.

He wrapped both hands around his shins. I caught the tremor rippling through his muscles. He was good at this all right. I almost had cause to wonder whether he'd played this game before.

Nix crawled down to join me at the bottom of the bed. He tipped a small amount of oil into his palm. "We should have brought a toy."

"A few hours ago, you were getting a divorce. You had no need of a toy."

"Oh, yes. I'd forgotten about that." He set two fingers to Piet's arsehole and thrust straight in to the second knuckle. Piet let out a sharp, shocked cry.

"How about a gag?"

"Do you have one of those at home in your toy box?"

"No." Nix pulled his glistening fingers back to the tips. "Piet got bored of playing sexual games with me. He prefers someone he can swap orgasms with."

Nix thrust his fingers back in, with no less speed than before. Only this time when I looked, there were three of them buried knuckle deep. "But it's different now you're playing with us, too."

He looked so utterly sexy with his fingers buried inside Piet's body. Before I could run through whether I was permitted or not, I clutched a handful of his hair and pushed my lips over his startled mouth.

After a moment of frozen shock, his lips started working against mine. He powered his tongue into my mouth and raked it across my back teeth. The heat of him sizzled with urgency, like a sex-starved lover, and yet that wasn't what Nix was. Affection-starved, possibly.

When I pulled back, he stared at me with heavy eyes. "I'm not Piet."

"I know." When I released him Nix continued to work his fingers in and out of Piet's arse, with slightly more finesse now. "Go back to two. All the way in and curl the tips. Find that spot inside him that makes him scream."

With an almost polite twist of his wrist, Nix thrust two fingers back inside. "Like this?"

Piet's back arched. "Oh. God." His hands left his shins and curled under the headboard. "Do that again." His words came out in desperate lurches. His cock, which he hadn't, to be fair, touched at all, practically glowed. A couple of drops of clear dew leaked onto his belly.

"Hold off a moment." I caught hold of Nix's wrist. His fingers were still buried deep inside Piet. The heat radiating from Piet's body sizzled through Nix's skin and burned my fingertips. I wondered what that heat would feel like radiating though my cock. I wanted to be there, in him. To the hilt. "He's close." I grasped the base of Piet's cock with my free hand. "I don't think it'll take much more than a couple of strokes."

When I swept my fist up his shaft, Piet ground down on Nix's fingers and tried to thrust at the same time. The harder he tried to get off on fucking Nix's fingers, the tighter I squeezed his cock.

"I think that's enough for him now." Nix withdrew his fingers as easily as he'd thrust them in, then wiped them clean with my discarded T-shirt. "Would you like me to suck your penis while Piet watches?"

"No. He wouldn't." Piet's voice was solid enough that I knew the subject wasn't ripe for negotiation. "The kiss was enough."

I could go along with that. I wasn't here to cause a rift. Just to try to heal one. "I think you should suck Piet's penis while I'm fucking him with mine. How does that sound?"

"If you think that's best." Nix offered out my shirt, now lube-streaked and aromatic with Piet's most intimate flavors. "Make Piet put the condom on you, though. He should have to do some things himself."

# Chapter Twenty-Six

"You heard what your hubby said." I dropped a condom onto Piet's belly. "Suit me up."

Piet glowered up at me. "I can always change my mind about this, you know."

"As can I." I repositioned myself with my back against the headboard and my feet straight out in front of me. As if there was any chance of me ever changing my mind.

"Hurry up before Dean gets bored." Nix handed Piet the lube. "Use some of this."

*Kid's a fast learner, that's for sure.*

Piet sat up. His fingers pressed tight around my shaft, closely followed by an even tighter skin of latex. He'd done this for me before, but this time he took a little more care and stroked my shaft to a lustful frenzy.

I clenched my fists, fighting off the urge to throw him face down on the bed and plunge deep into his well-lubed hole.

*Not about me.* That was the one thing I had to keep reminding myself. "Sit on my thighs but facing Nix."

"And what if I don't want to?"

"Then I get dressed and go home." Like fuck I would, but I was hoping the possibility might shut down any future objections.

Piet scanned my expression, but I kept any trace of the lie off my face. "You'll have to guide me down," he said as he climbed onto my thighs and presented me with his snowy arse. "I can't see much of anything from here."

"Not without your glasses, hey?"

As he knelt, I slipped a hand to his hips to guide him down. One of my thumbs may have quite accidently slipped into the crack of his arse and followed the greasy track of lube down to his opening. That same thumb may have, also quite by accident, eased inside.

Piet whimpered but disguised the whimper by clearing his throat. "Is that your dick?"

Ah, so he wasn't done with his special brand of humor just yet.

"Don't talk," Nix said, from the foot of the bed. "You're spoiling it."

Piet lowered his knees to the mattress, thighs spread either side of mine.

I withdrew my thumb and slipped my hand round Piet's warm belly. I nudged him back against me until his entrance lined up to my cock.

When Piet was halfway to seat on my full length, I wrapped my other hand around his waist. Greedy for that final nudge of heat, I thrust up with my hips.

Piet yelped. He sank forwards, hands on my thighs, shuddering for breath.

I nuzzled my lips across his ear. "Can we quit with the size jokes now?"

"Fuck." He sucked in air though his teeth. "You."

I switched my attention to Nix, who was watching us from the foot of the bed. "Your husband's talking again. What you going to do about it?"

"Well. I could stuff some underpants in his mouth. Yours and mine. He does have a very big mouth."

I buried a laugh in Piet's naked shoulder. "I was thinking more of your tongue."

Nix sighed. "That would be better, I suppose." He didn't sound convinced. All this talk of blindfolds and underwear for gags—he'd been reading far too many kinky books.

"Come on, then," I said, before he got any other ideas. Like ropes and whips. Although I wasn't entirely opposed to tying Piet up, I had better things to do to him. "I'll hold him still." I dropped one hand to Piet's cock, the other under his balls.

Nix rose on his knees and eased along the mattress either side of my shins. I had no idea if he was hard under those voluminous pajamas, or what he'd want done about it if he was. Probably nothing. All he seemed to want was to make Piet's experience a good one.

Piet grabbed hold of him, a hand each side of his face, and engulfed him in a kiss. Nix floundered before finding his balance. He slid both arms around Piet's back and held on as Piet sucked the life out of him. No one had kissed me with that much passion in my entire life. I could only hope to experience that fevered lust for another person one day.

I pushed my back against the solid headboard and thrust my hips. My cock was a raw nerve enveloped in a soft, frantic heat. I held on to his hips while he rode me, his mouth full of Nix, his arse full of me. Low grunts throbbed deep in his throat and matched the short rasps puffing through my lungs.

Nix pulled away from the kiss. He sank down, almost as if he'd fallen. Then I clocked what he was doing. A startled yelp came from Piet and a shudder that vibrated from him all the way along my cock.

Nix had taken Piet in his mouth.

I pushed forward for a better view and caught the blond roots and the top of Nix's bobbing head as his lips rode their path along Piet's naked shaft.

"Oh God! Please." Piet locked his hands in Nix's hair. He threw himself back against me, the rear of his skull just shy of ramming into my teeth. "Fuck me. Both of you. Hard."

We were doing our best.

I clung to his hips, catching his rhythm as I pumped up into him and he in turn ground down on me. I leaned forward and licked the curve of his spine. He tasted of arousal and the faintest trace of salt. Together we chased desires with the heavy beat of our breaths, the harsh bounce of the bed and the soft slurps of Nix's mouth.

When Piet arched with a frantic buck of his hips, a low groan rolled from his throat. The air filled with the harsh glug of Nix swallowing him down.

"Jesus." My arousal shivered through me. I wrapped my arms around Piet's belly and pumped up into him twice more. His arse clamped down, sealing me inside. All the fire trapped in my balls expelled, pulsing thick waves through my cock. I came hard, exploding into Piet's body.

My muscles seized and light flashed in my head, blinding and warming. I fell back heavily into the headboard, panting hard. "That was…"

"Yes," Piet muttered, resting his head back on my shoulder.

I closed my eyes and coasted. When I came to, Nix was sat up and staring at me. His hair hung into his eyes. His cum-sheened lips tilted. Not quite a smile.

"That was the best time Piet's ever had," he announced. How he could be so certain I didn't know, but Piet didn't pose any objection. He was halfway to dozing off and using me as his bed.

"Come here." I tugged Nix close and lunged forward and pushed my tongue into his mouth. Piet's flavors, ripe and salty, mixed with Nix's own sweetness.

"We have to do this again," Nix said, breaking the kiss. He vibrated with excitement, which was odd for someone who appeared to be entirely asexual. But I couldn't pretend to understand how it all worked. I only knew how I worked. With these two, I worked very well.

"Is it okay if I take a breather first? Piet will be quick to tell you, I'm not as young as he is."

"Hmm." Piet wrapped his arms around Nix and hugged him close as a teddy bear. "Shut up, Dean."

"You two aren't going to fall asleep on me, are you?" As tempting as the thought of curling up with the two of them was, it wasn't how I planned on spending what was left of the day.

"We're resting," Piet said, through a yawn. "Which is something your voice hasn't had enough of."

*Sarky fuck.*

# Chapter Twenty-Seven

They did move, eventually, and arranged themselves either side of me on the bed. Nix wouldn't let me move. Not even to flush the condom. He allotted Piet the honor instead. Maybe he thought now I'd got mine, I'd run.

*No chance.*

I enjoyed having them close, their heads resting on my chest, a hand each on my belly and cock. I couldn't even tell who had what on where under the covers until one warm hand slid away and Nix rolled onto his back.

"What are you doing?" Piet lifted his head, eyelids drooping. His cock wasn't drooping, though. He had a semi pressed to my hip.

Nix wriggled around under the covers. "I'm taking my clothes off."

I looked at him. "Why?" I never knew what Nix's motives were, but he never failed to surprise me.

"Because you two are naked." He dropped his pajama bottoms over the side of the bed. "I don't want to be different."

"You, my friend, will always be different."

"Dean." Piet's hand tightened on my cock, a touch the wrong side of firm.

"Would you quit that?" I placed my hand over his. "I didn't mean anything negative. I'm not even talking about the sex thing."

"Well. I suppose that's all right then." Piet returned his cheek to my chest. His grip eased on my cock but didn't fall away.

Nix slipped out of his top, although he remained engulfed by the duvet, then resumed snuggling by at my side. "Now we're all the same."

I stroked the bony plane of his hip still covered by his underpants. Not quite the same as naked, but that he'd done this purely of his own accord warmed me as much as our physical closeness. And with me so sated and content, my thoughts drifted. Wasn't this every non-straight guy's fantasy?

Piet slid a leg over my thigh and pushed his palm across my belly. "You're quiet."

"Yeah. I'm thinking."

"What about?"

I considered not telling him, but since he'd asked, it was my duty. "If the three of us were in a porno, what would it be called?"

Piet lifted his head. "Do you always have to say the inanest things that run through your mind?"

"Nope. I'm usually good at censoring myself, but since you asked what I was thinking, *Two Twinks, One Todger*."

"What?"

"The name of our movie."

"Todger or Tosser?"

"Todger. No question. Because I haven't got around to toss—"

Nix raised his head. "What's a twink?"

Now I had the pair of them gawping at me.

"Never mind." Piet poked me in the ribs. "Dean's being an idiot."

I still wasn't sure whether Nix was capable of winding anyone up, but that last question couldn't be genuine. *Could it?* "Come on. You must know what a twink is."

"He means us." Piet gifted me with another disapproving glare. "He sees us as his toys."

"I don't." That wasn't what I'd meant. I suspected he knew that and was looking for trouble for the sake of it.

"What do you see us as then?" I wasn't sure how much Piet could see without his glasses, but that look cut right through me.

"Shouldn't you be asking what you two are to yourselves?" Fuck, I sounded like one of those self-help nutcases on daytime TV.

"We know what we are." Nix's fingers found my nipple and pinched. "We're married."

A hot spark seared through my chest. I gritted my teeth. "I am aware of that. But you two need to talk. And while you do that, I thought I'd..." The pinch softened to a roll between forefinger and thumb.

"Thought you'd what?" Piet's voice was tight.

Distracted by the little burst of heat that tingled all the way from nipple to balls, I lost my train of thought. *Train. That was it.* "I thought I'd go home. Give you two some alone time to talk."

"You're not leaving." Nix pushed his leg across my thigh. "You're staying the night. You're invited."

"He's got what he wanted from us." Piet unstuck himself from my sweat-slicked skin. "There's no need for him to hang around any longer."

"What was it that you think I wanted?" I thought I'd been clear on that for a while now.

"Sex." Nix peered down at me, although his leg remained spread across my thigh and his arm across my belly. "Do you?"

"Want to leave? No. But you two still need to talk. To decide where it is I fit in. And I don't mean that in the physical sense, before one of you states the obvious."

"The obvious what?"

"We've already decided," Piet said, from all the way across the bed. "Don't make up excuses. If you want to leave, leave."

"What did you decide?" I asked, because I'd been with them all this time and no such discussion had taken place.

Piet sat up. The sheet settled around his hips. "Are you stupid? Did you get the impression we hated every moment of what happened between us?"

"No. You liked it pretty good." I turned to Nix. "Although I don't know how much you got out of it."

"Piet's orgasm. He's never had one like that before."

"Yes, I have. With you."

"He hasn't." Nix addressed me. "He just doesn't want to admit that he was wrong."

This was interesting. "What was he wrong about?"

"You," Piet said, with a dismissive wave. "Or I should say I was right all along."

"If you were right, then you weren't wrong," I said, applying a little of Nix's simple logic. "All I know is this was all going along swimmingly when you were sat on my cock."

"And when I had him in my mouth," Nix agreed, with a little nod.

"Yes, and now that's over, Dean wants to leave." Piet pushed back the covers and swung his legs out of bed. "Don't let us stop you."

"I'm stopping him." Nix dived over me, pushing his near-naked body over mine, like two slices of bread in a sandwich with our cocks as the filling. "Now you can't leave."

# Chapter Twenty-Eight

"What are you planning?" I cupped Nix's arse cheeks, which were toasty warm through his briefs. "Staying on top all night? Because that's more than fine by me." My cock appreciated his heat and his proximity, briefs or no briefs.

His arse twitched under my palms. "It'll be dinnertime soon."

"So?"

"So I'm hungry. Piet will have to take my place."

Piet pulled on his jeans. "I'm not the one who wants him to stay."

"Yes, you are," Nix said. "Take his clothes. He can't leave naked."

"You want me to stay that bad, huh?" I tickled my fingers up his spine. "You reckon Piet does, too?"

"Of course. But he won't say so."

I pushed my mouth to Nix's ear. He smelled warm and faintly perfumed. "Get him to say so, and I'll stay."

Nix turned to his husband. "Did you hear what Dean said?"

Piet collected his T-shirt off the floor and put it on. "He wants me to beg, and I'm not going to do that."

"But I've asked you to stay." Nix frowned down at me. "That should be enough."

"It's fifty percent enough," I said, trying to remain calm and rational, all the while ignoring the heat of Nix tingling over my skin. "And I don't want him to beg. Just to ask."

"Why?"

I met Piet's gaze. "Because I need to know how you feel about me. If I'm going to be allowed to develop feelings as well as a hard-on for you two, I'll need some real reassurances back."

"You mean you're capable of experiencing more than a hard-on for a couple of twinks starring in your own private porno fantasies?"

*Ah, so that's where I went wrong. Some things really are best kept private.* "That's nothing like how I see you two," I said, reminding myself that neither of these two lads had much of a sense of humor. "I want us to see where the three of us can take this relationship. Because I'll call it that if you will."

Piet folded his arms. "A relationship would mean you'd have to stop fucking all those other people at the holiday park."

"I already did. The day I met you."

He studied my face, seeking the lie he wouldn't find. "Are you capable of an exclusive relationship?"

"I'm capable of doing whatever it takes if the result is us three. Together."

"I believe him." Nix peered into my face. "I knew he'd be perfect."

"He's hardly perfect." Piet was never going to let such a compliment slip by. "But if he can keep his promise not to sleep around on us, he'll do for now."

"Works both ways, too," I told him. And he thought he had won with the sneaky addition of that 'for now'. "No more five-minute shagging sessions with whoever takes your fancy at work."

"You don't have to worry about that," Nix said. "He's banned from having sex with anyone else."

"I am?" Piet climbed back on the bed, kneeling at our side. "When did you decide this?"

"The day Dean turned up at home." Nix slid off me and settled at my side. "I've also decided that as you've been incredibly rude, you're going to have to make it up to him."

"I haven't been rude." Piet scowled at me. "He made up a porn title for us."

"But you like porn. You should be pleased."

Piet started to say something then shook his head. "Never mind. What do I have to do?"

"That's easy." Nix sat up, keeping the sheet pinned to his chest. He grabbed a handful of the sheet covering me and yanked it from my body. "He has an erection. He'd like you to see to it with your mouth."

Not a single puff escaped my lips. There was no way I was going to jeopardize my chances.

Piet flushed in the soft, virginal hue that had first drawn me to him. "I only do that for you."

"And I didn't like it," Nix announced, with his usual lack of anything resembling diplomacy. "Besides which, you haven't used your mouth on me in years."

"Or on anyone else," Piet said quietly. "Ever."

My cock jerked to full attention. I hadn't even gone near it with my hand, but the thought of me being Piet's first ever blowjob, not counting Nix, had me sliding my free hand toward my shaft for a quick fumble.

"I'm sure Dean won't mind having his penis in your mouth. Even if he doesn't want to put it in mine."

I bit my tongue. Mostly because if it were up to me, I would've invited Nix to give me a demonstration of his talents. But I'd always put Piet's wishes above my own. I guessed that was how relationships worked.

"Why do I have to do it?" Piet asked, like sucking my dick was an evil punishment. Didn't stop him from ogling when I skimmed my fingers along my shaft.

"Because I want to watch you do all the things you can't do with me, with Dean." Nix brushed my hand away from my dick then clasped a fist around the base. The shock made me gasp, despite my vow of silence. "Do it now, Piet. You know he won't last long."

*What am I, a slab of raw meat left out too long in the sun?*

"I'm not happy," Piet said, despite the fact that he was shuffling closer. About to lean over my cock. "Just so you're aware."

"Wait!" Nix unclamped his fist and pressed his palm over my erection. Like a padlock. The difference in pressure had me lurching under his palm. A flurry of heat burned deep in my balls, and I couldn't help but nudge into his touch. "You have to take off your clothes first."

"What?" Piet jerked back. He'd been about to take me in his mouth, and now I wished Nix would shut the fuck up. "I've only just got dressed."

"I'm naked. Dean's naked. That means you have to be naked, too."

Piet shot me a glare. As if I'd made the whole nakedness thing my rule. I didn't give a fuck how he did this, as long as he did. A fitting dessert following a delightful main course.

He whipped off his T-shirt. "I bet you're loving this."

I turned to Nix. I couldn't help myself. "Can we do the whole 'Piet not talking' thing again? Works so much better that way."

"I agree." Nix rubbed his palm along my length. "Although he won't be able to talk at all when he has this massive thing down his throat."

*Massive thing.* I liked Nix's pillow talk more and more. And the delicate way his hand slid along my shaft had me shivering with arousal all the same.

"He's not that massive," Piet said, unfastening his fly.

"He's bigger than you." Nix withdrew his palm. "Look at it."

*From slab of meat to freak show attraction in the space of a few minutes.* Boredom was never going to be a factor with these two, that was for sure.

Piet paused with his jeans pushed to his hips. "He's adequate."

"He gives you good orgasms."

Piet didn't disagree with him.

"Hurry up," Nix said, as Piet pulled off the last of his clothing. "Cinder could be back at any moment and you need to see to him before dinnertime."

I'd forgotten about Cinder. And dinner. And anyone or anything who wasn't in this bed. Even Brian, who'd probably got us both fired for lamping an awkward customer at the clubhouse by now. But those things I'd worry about later.

Piet leaned over me once again, this time taking my cock in his fist and dipping out his tongue. He pressed the tip to my shaft and trailed a warm line of saliva over my foreskin.

Nix's lips landed on mine just as Piet's lips sealed the head of my cock in velvet.

And this, this was just the beginning…

# Epilogue

*Two months later*

"So, there was a someone?" Piet asked. His eyes were hazy from orgasm, but his curiosity held my gaze.

We were naked, in my bed, barely two minutes from an exhaustive fuck, and all I wanted to do was doze. Instead Piet had chosen now to ask the questions he'd ventured twice before — using different words, but the gist remained the same. Had I ever had a serious relationship? The previous two times he'd asked, I'd dodged the answer entirely. Today, I wasn't going to dodge. Mainly because we were in my bed, and the question wasn't going anywhere. Also because there was something extra comfortable about a thorough shagging session in my own home.

"Once. A long time ago."

Piet resettled his head on my chest. "Tell me about her. I'm assuming it was a her?"

"Her name was — and I guess, still is — Trudy."

"Who's Trudy?" Nix chose that moment to stroll in, clad in his usual too-big pajamas and armed with a tub of ice cream and a spoon. For someone who was so skinny and ill, he put away a lot of sugar.

"Someone Dean used to know."

Nix pried the lid from the tub, then took a seat next to me on the bed. "You mean the married woman he had an affair with?"

"An affair?" Piet sat up. "You told Nix this and not me?"

"You've always been too busy having sex with him to actually talk to him. Whereas Dean and I have conversations. Lots of them. Some even about you."

I could almost hear each individual hair spike on Piet's skin. "What have you said about me?"

"No worse than what you've said about me." This could get out of hand quickly if these two started kicking off on each other. They bickered rather than outright argued, and most of the time the bickering was quite purposefully instigated by Nix.

"I won't even ask about that." Piet swiped a full spoonful of ice cream from Nix's hand. "Who was she, then, this Trudy?" He pushed the spoon into his mouth and sucked away the contents.

He didn't need to panic. I could um and ah about who Trudy had been or who she was to me now, but since I was going to tell this story, I'd give it to him straight. "She was my mother's best friend. And a receptionist here for a while. We hooked up a few times over the course of a summer. I haven't seen her in years. Wouldn't know how to find her even if I wanted to."

Piet handed the spoon back to Nix. "Why would you want to?"

I didn't miss the ice in the question. It had nothing to do with the chill of the ice cream. "I've thought about it, a time or two. I guess I'm curious."

"About her?"

"Not so much her." He wanted to know about my past—I'd serve him up a great big slice of it. A risk, yeah, but we all had our skeletons. "I think I'd like to know about my kid."

The resulting silence was the first I'd heard in quite a while. Both Piet and Nix looked at each other as though I'd vanished into the ether.

"Is it one of his jokes?" Nix leaned across me to speak directly to his husband. "They're never funny."

"I don't think so." Piet looked at me. "Are you joking?"

I shook my head.

"So." Piet hefted in a deep breath. "You have a child? Where?"

"I don't know."

"You can't misplace a baby." Nix dug out another spoonful of ice cream. "That would definitely be illegal."

"Trudy has the baby," I said. "But since I don't know where she is, how the fuck should I know where the kid is?"

Piet's eyebrows lifted. "Are you aware of how indifferent you sound? About your own child?"

He had judged me and found me lacking. Maybe this was the very reason I'd been reluctant to talk about my past in the first place. "It's hard to care about a kid I've never seen."

"You must care because you're talking about it," Nix said, with his unique brand of logic.

I shrugged. "You asked."

"Piet asked."

"Yeah. And now I've told you both."

Piet ran a hand though his hair. "When did all this happen?"

"Years ago."

"How many?"

Didn't take a moment to count back through. "Five."

"Your baby is five years old?"

"Four. More kid than baby."

"And you've never even met?"

"Nope." I'd always pictured him as blond, like Trudy. And a bit of a handful, like me. I'd heard fourth- or fifth-hand that she'd had a boy. There was no point in questioning my mother. She refused to acknowledge she even had a grandkid. "According to anyone I ever had cause to ask, I've got no right to meet him."

"Of course you have rights. You're the baby's father."

"No. I was a stupid kid who believed she was on the pill." I didn't plan the bitterness. I was beyond that now, or thought I was. I should have been beyond this story, but Piet had insisted he wanted the secret he was convinced I was keeping from them. Now he had it. Looking at his face, I think he wished he didn't. "Her husband couldn't have kids. They'd tried IVF with no success. Then me and her started sleeping together and a few months later she's pregnant."

"Was she your first?" Curiosity softened Piet's tone. I might even have detected a touch of empathy there, too.

I snorted out a laugh. "No. My first was a long time before Trudy. But I was seventeen, and the lure of an older woman was too much to resist. She taught me a few things I—"

"We don't need that much detail," Piet said quickly.

"I do." Nix set down the ice-cream tub and fixed me with his full attention. "What did she teach you, exactly?"

Nix wasn't stupid, so I had to wonder if these whacked-up questions were genuine or something he said for effect. But if there was any hint he was winding me up, I never saw so much as a twitch of mirth flicker across his face.

"The whole thing ended up destroying the friendship my mum and Trudy had. What was left of any relationship I had with my parents, too."

Piet covered my hand in his, or half-covered since his were smaller. I guess this was him in sympathetic mode, but at least he wasn't blaming me for the sorry mess like everyone else had. "Does Trudy's husband assume the child is his?"

"They'd been trying for years without success, then suddenly she gets pregnant? He'd have to be pretty gullible to believe it could be his."

"It explains a lot about you."

"Does it?" I was desperate for a cigarette I knew I couldn't have.

"Yes. I understand now why you reacted how you did with Nix and me." He bit his lip. "We'd never have asked you if we'd known."

"Then I'm glad you didn't know. Because I wouldn't be without this." I took their hands, one in each of mine. "I wouldn't have trusted anyone else with the two of you."

"I'd have still asked." Nix pressed his lips to mine. A warm, gentle kiss designed for what? Comfort? He wrapped an arm around my chest and leaned his cheek into my naked shoulder. "You would have made a good father if you'd been given the chance."

I hadn't been expecting that. Nix liked to kiss, but he wasn't the touchy-feely or sympathetic type. "The chances are I wouldn't." I pulled back from his embrace. "I thought you were the realist in this relationship."

Nix tilted his head. "Was the reason you had sex with all those girls at the park to get another baby?"

This was more like it. Direct questions that followed no rhyme or reason and about as tactful as a sledgehammer. "No. I definitely don't want babies."

"It's a bit late for that." Piet sighed. "You already have at least one."

I leaned back against the headboard wishing we could draw this conversation to an end sooner rather than later. "No more babies, then. I don't even like kids."

"Don't you?" Nix sounded surprised, like I was committing a criminal offense with my confession. I doubted he'd spent any significant time with kids to make any judgment on me.

"No, but if that's your thing, you go right ahead and make a few." I caught Piet's eye. He had that face on. The starched expression reserved especially for when I said something to Nix that could be construed as ridiculing him. "I think we're all good as we are, aren't we? Just me and you two."

"I suppose." Nix spooned out another chunk of ice cream. "Why did you get vanilla when you must know by now I prefer strawberry?"

"I wasn't aware I had to change my taste to suit yours."

"You also didn't want to get involved with married people, but here you are with us."

"He's got a point." Piet lay down, the tension bleeding away.

I dropped my gaze to the tented sheet. "You too."

"Are you going to have sex yet again?" Nix asked. He'd never been that interested in joining us as he had that first time the three of us had gotten together.

"Yes," I said.

"No." Piet brought the sheet up over his chest. "We're going to sleep."

"In that case, I'll join you." Nix set down the tub and the spoon, then wiped his mouth with his pajama sleeve.

He climbed over my thighs, then settled himself into the center between Piet and me. "By the way," he said to me, while making himself comfortable. "We're staying over again tonight."

"You are?" I didn't mind, but Piet had work, so he might. I waited for him to object. To say something like, he couldn't possibly stay two nights in a row — he had to go and fetch his work uniform and check the gas meter, or some such excuse.

When Piet added nothing to Nix's announcement, I let myself relax.

There was every probability right now that the three of us together were going to be okay.

# Want to see more from this author? Here's a taster for you to enjoy!

# Rent Mate
## Ash Penn

### *Excerpt*

Liam West had just finished a ten-hour stint at the hospital and wanted nothing more than to crawl into bed and cocoon himself under the duvet for the next week. But first he had to speak with Katie. What had happened between them yesterday afternoon had nagged at him all the way through the night shift. So much so, he'd lost his temper at a couple of drunken revelers who'd turned up at A&E bruised and bloodied as a result of a fight. Prior to that, he'd had to wheel a twenty-year-old girl to the morgue.

After putting the kettle on, he went to Katie's door and tapped rather than knocked. Anything to avoid the wrath of Martin, who hated to be woken before ten. Woe betide anyone who interrupted his beauty sleep. Not that he needed much, the vain little shit.

"Katie? Can we talk?"

No answer.

It occurred to him then that when she'd stormed out yesterday afternoon she might not have come back. She'd already stayed out four of the last five nights, so one more wouldn't make any difference. He knocked again, harder. "Katie? You awake?"

Silence.

Liam opened the door.

Sunlight seeped around the partially open blinds and threw a sharp beam across the bed. Highlighted in this radiant glow was the flutter of golden eyelashes spread upon a pale cheek. Beneath a button nose, full lips rested together and formed a petulant pout that may or may not have been the result of collagen injections.

*Wait a minute.*

What was he doing staring at Martin Bailey's lips? Especially when those lips were pouting in his best friend's bed. Liam forged inside the room, ready to eject the bastard short shrift. Then the golden lashes flickered open.

Martin lifted his arms in a lazy stretch. The move elongated his torso, displaying the fine arc of his ribs and the smooth dip of his taut belly. From there Liam's attention was drawn to where the covers met his groin.

*Wait another minute.*

Was he *naked* under that quilt?

"Liam?" Martin slurred, suggesting he'd been in the midst of a deep sleep. "What're you doing here?"

"You're starkers in Katie's bed, and you ask me what *I'm* doing here?"

"Katie's..." Martin looked blearily around. "Oh. Hell." He pushed the quilt aside and swung his legs out of the far side of the bed.

Liam flipped on the light.

Martin threw an arm across his eyes. "Man. You have to do that?"

"Yes." Liam clenched his teeth. "Why are you in here? What's wrong with your own bed? And where's Katie?"

Ignoring every question, Martin stood and stretched both arms high above his head. As he did so, Liam's gaze fell to the small, pert peach of his backside. Dark patches bloomed on the pale skin, harsh blobs that looked very much like finger-shaped bruises. "Have you had someone here?" he asked the bruises. "A…" What were they called? Customers? Clients? *Johns?* "A punter?" Liam clung to the word with both hands. "You had a punter in here?"

Martin didn't laugh at the term, but neither did he offer up an answer. Instead, he bent to pick up his clothing as if Liam had ceased to exist. As he did so he let out a pained groan and pressed a palm to his belly.

"What's wrong?" Liam asked, knowing he shouldn't give a shit. Especially after finding the bastard in his best friend's bed. But he couldn't ignore the fact Martin was in pain. And considering those bruises, and what he did for a living, Martin's pain must get pretty bad at times.

"Nothing." Martin straightened, using the bed post as support. "It's just the bloke from last night." His blue eyes shimmered from under a mop of tousled hair.

Liam's rage dissolved. What the hell had gone on in here? "What happened, Martin? You can tell me." He edged another step closer. "Did he hurt you? Or…?" Or worse?

"He…" Martin sucked in another sharp breath. "God, Liam. He…" His plump lower lip trembled, then parted from his equally plump top lip to form a manic grin. "He's got a cracking great knob on him. Knows how to make thorough use of it, too. My arse is flaming like a Catherine wheel on bonfire night."

Every bit of sympathy Liam held in his body boiled away. "You are a sick, fucking…"

Martin let out a cackle of ear-grating laughter then reached under the pillow. He spun around, waving a shock of notes in the air. "Not bad for half an hour's graft, eh?"

Half an hour? The steam from Liam's anger thinned to disbelief. There was as much there as he earned in a week. How fair was that? Then again, thinking back to the bruises, the money wasn't so great.

"Where is she?" Liam asked as his temperature once again set to simmer.

"Who?"

"Katie. Who'd you think?"

"I reckon she spent the night with her boyfriend. Her well fit boyfriend, from what I saw."

"You've *met* him?" That Katie had broken her promise to stay home last night was bad enough, but paled into insignificance when contrasted with the fact that Martin had met this elusive new bloke of hers.

"Yeah." Martin idly flicked through his takings. "Why?"

Liam paused. He refused to show just how much of a slap in the face that was. "So while she's out you thought you'd, what? Take advantage of her absence? You really are pathetic." Liam itched to shake a sense of decency into the little shit. But there wasn't much to grab a hold of except his half-erect cock, and Liam was keeping well out of the way of that thing. "I want you out of here. Now!"

"All right, big man." Martin raised a dismissive palm. "No need for the 'tude." He set about gathering the rest of his clothing from the floor, then paused in the doorway on his way out. "You reckon you could give the sheets a rinse through? They're a little…crusty."

Liam surged toward him, fists clenched, but being twice Martin's size meant an unfair advantage right from the off. And since Liam despised violence more than he despised Martin, he stood there and seethed instead while Martin continued down the hall like nothing was up other than his dick.

"And I mean out," Liam yelled, trying not to stare at the pert cheeks of that perfect, if bruised, arse. Out of the flat and out of their lives. For good.

"Then have a word with Katie." Martin flashed another exaggerated grin from over his shoulder. "It's got to be unanimous, or I'm going *no*where." He disappeared into his room then, and slammed the door behind him.

Martin placed his earnings into his night-table drawer then lowered himself gingerly to the bed. Falling asleep in Katie's bed had been a mistake, a big one. He'd only used her room because pink suited his alter-ego's personality. Feminine, chic fairy lights and a patchwork quilt beat wallpaper made of porn stills and the half bottle of whiskey sitting on his chest of drawers.

As he made to rise from the bed, he caught his reflection in the full-length mirror hanging on the door. Martin Bailey — all bedhead and bloodshot eyes. But if he fluffed up his blond hair and lowered his lashes, if he parted his lips and licked them until they glistened, then there was Button. The sweetly innocent sap hardly clued in about sex, and forever oblivious of the effect his young body had on the men who were willing to pay to explore it. The kid Roy wanted to buy and keep purely for pleasure.

Like that was going to happen. He couldn't play the naïve piece of fluff twenty-four-seven. Mainly because his pathetic alter-ego's saccharine willingness to please pissed him off no end. He'd taken his frustration out on Liam this morning and now would have to heal the atmosphere. He liked living here, more than most of the other places he'd stayed. But before he did anything else today, he needed that shower.

Standing under the hot water jets, he cleansed the grime of his job with a generous slather of Katie's strawberry shower gel. She never minded him using her things, unlike Liam staring daggers across the Weetabix of a morning. Liam minded he dare breathe half the time. Granted, breakfast was usually dinner time for them both, but, no matter what time of the day or night, the sad fact was he and Liam would never become friends.

He'd grown to appreciate the big guy over the past few months of living here, despite the constant complaints and not-so-subtle digs about his job. However hard he tried, he wouldn't be able to wear an eternal grin for minimum wage in a supermarket. He could smile for a two hundred quid shag, no problem. He could please any man on a fifty quid blow job. He'd perfected the art in cheap hotel rooms and narrow alleyways for going on almost three years now, and before then in the privacy of his home.

Not all his punters were totally undesirable, either. Roy had his good points. He was never violent or overtly kinky. He insisted on bringing Button to orgasm every single time. A lot of others weren't so generous. Even so, last night Roy had become extra pushy, extra keen to claim Button's flesh as his own.

After switching off the water, Martin wrapped a towel around his waist. Bath rather than hand. Usually he'd deliberately parade around in a much smaller towel just to flaunt himself in Liam's company. Irritating the big guy had proven to be quite the leisure pursuit lately. Precisely the reason he'd not-so-casually dropped meeting Katie's latest boyfriend into the conversation. In reality, their introduction had been little more than a brief hi and bye when passing in the hall, but Liam didn't need to know that.

Martin grabbed his toothbrush and scrubbed the remnants of Roy's taste from his mouth, then made his way through to the kitchen. Liam was sitting at the table nursing a coffee. He might be fuming like a midsummer's dung heap, but he smelled much nicer. Sweaty but clean, with a frisson of some ocean-themed aftershave. Aesthetically, he wasn't too bad on the eye, either. Tall, broad and black-haired, he exuded a soothing presence. A quiet, underlying strength, a protective presence that Martin liked. A lot. Mainly because Liam was totally straight and remained so even when wasted. Every now and then, though, Martin liked to wobble the boundaries to see how safe his walls were. The reason he found Liam's smoldering presence quite so warming was best pondered another day.

He set five crisp ten-pound notes on the table then pulled out a chair. Perhaps he should have dressed first, but this bad atmosphere needed tackling sooner rather than later.

Liam eyed the notes. "What's this?"

"An apology." Martin fixed on his brightest grin. "I shouldn't have taken Katie's bed, and this is my way of saying sorry."

"Fifty quid's worth of sorry?" Liam swept the cash to the floor. "I'm not your pimp, Martin. You can't pay me to keep my mouth shut, either." He powered to his feet. Fists pushed to the table, knuckles big as bolts. "In fact, I've got a good mind to show you exactly what I think of you."

"Go ahead." Martin pushed back his chair and stood, too. "I can take a fist. Just be aware I charge an extra hundred for the privilege." He stuck out his chin and readied for the glancing blow he probably deserved. Not that he believed Liam would cave his face in, bolt knuckles or no bolt knuckles. Liam just wasn't the violent type. His gamble paid off when Liam slumped in his chair and picked up his mug.

"Will you tell Katie?" Martin resumed his seat. His adrenaline fizzled to a sickly slither of nerves. Katie wouldn't want him to leave, would she? She was an easy-going girl, but there had to be a limit to even her level of acceptance. Using her bed to entertain his clients wouldn't go down well, no matter how close their friendship.

Liam hunched his shoulders. "Depends."

"On what?"

"The reason you did it."

*Like that's any of Liam's business.* "One of my regulars wanted to see where I live. He's been hassling me for exclusive use, and I—"

"Exclusive use? What does that mean?"

"Just that he wants to buy me. Like, full-time. So I'd get to be with him and no one else."

"You mean he wants to *own* you?"

"No way. I ain't nobody's slave." Martin scowled. "I just thought if he could see that I don't live in squalor with a bunch of junkies and rapists, he'd stop worrying about my living conditions and—"

"You could've used your room for that. You could've made do with a single. In the past I've had to..." Liam shut his mouth.

"You've had to what?"

"Nothing." Liam dragged his mug closer. "We're talking about your bedroom habits here, not mine."

Only because Liam probably didn't even have any bedroom habits. Not past his right hand, anyway. For as long as they'd known each other, Liam had never brought anyone back to shag. He'd never brought anyone back, ever.

"Roy — that's my punter — he clocked the naked meat pinned to my door and wasn't impressed. So I had to tell him my room was my flatmate's, AKA, yours."

Liam spluttered a mouthful of coffee halfway across the table. "You told your trick that porn infested hell-hole was *mine?*"

"You mind?"

"Of course I mind, dipshit." Liam pushed out of the chair and fetched some kitchen towel from the roll on the wall. "Like anyone is going to believe you kip in a pink fairy grotto, anyway." He swiped the towel across the puddle but only succeeded in spreading it further. "You're not that camp."

"I ain't camp, full stop." Martin bit down on his anger. Trying to communicate with Liam was a total waste of time, as always. But he owed an explanation. Wouldn't be an acceptable one, but it would be the truth. "I'm not. But Button is."

Liam paused his mopping. "Who's Button?"

"Me. Sort of. He's, like, a persona. Button's seventeen. A dumb twink who swaps bum fun for cash 'cause he's too thick to work a proper job."

"Sounds like you, never mind this Button character." He deposited the soggy towel in the bin. "Apart from you being twenty-one and a long way from dumb, that is."

He'd take that as a compliment, even if dumb probably referred to his mouth rather than his intelligence. "Yeah, well, in my line of work, the younger and more inexperienced you appear the more you can charge and the more the blokes are willing to pay. They lap it up, trust me."

"I don't doubt it." Liam shot him another disapproving look before sitting back down. "How old are they, then? These blokes who pay fake seventeen-year-olds for sex. What about him last night?"

"Dunno. Sixtyish."

"Sixtyish?" Liam's disgust flared again, in full uniform regalia of the likes not seen since some passing neighbor had thrown up in the hall directly outside their front door. "You bring sick old fucks who like teenage boys to mine and Katie's home, then give them what they want in Katie's bed?"

The earlier compliment meant absolutely nothing if Liam thought this of him now. "I only brought Roy back, and he ain't even that sick a fuck." Roy treated him with respect. Roy also fucked hard enough to bruise, but the bruises were of the energetic, not the violent, variety. "Seventeen is legal. I could play younger if I wanted, but I got my principles, too."

Liam snorted out a laugh.

Martin chose to ignore it. "Roy's harmless enough and he tips well."

"Yeah, well. Whatever he is or isn't" — Liam stabbed a finger down on the table — "you bring any more of your desperado perverts here, and I will throw you out myself. Personally. Rental agreement or no rental agreement. Understood?"

"Sure. I get it." Martin slipped from the chair to the floor and set about gathering his money together. He stuffed the cash into his pocket then levered himself upright. A fresh spark of fire seared through his pelvis and he couldn't prevent a whimper that made Liam's upper lip curl in distaste. Now there was an expression he'd caught on a variety of different faces over the years, and was more than used to ignoring. "Time I was going, anyway. There's a half price breakfast down the pub with my name on it."

PUBLISHING

Sign up for our newsletter and find out about all our
romance book releases, eBook sales and promotions,
sneak peeks and FREE romance eBooks!

https://totallyentwinedgroup.us7.list-
manage.com/subscribe/post

# About the Author

I've written stories about men loving men for as long as I can remember. In the days before computers and the internet, I used to hide my stories away convinced there was no market for women who wrote gay male fiction. Fast forward a few years (okay, quite a few years) and there's not only a market, but a whole empire out there for writers like me. I'm thrilled to be able to contribute my stories and take pride in what I write.

Many of my characters enjoy making my life as difficult as possible by refusing to take the easy pathway to love. They prefer to swagger through the undergrowth and laugh at me as I point at my story outline and demand they get back on the route I painstakingly mapped out.

Lately I've discovered it's far easier to let them dictate what happens and when, although I do get my revenge when it comes to giving them an undesirable trait or two to contend with. My characters are as flawed as their love lives, but they will usually find a kind of imperfect perfection in each other by the time I type 'The End'.

Ash loves to hear from readers. You can find her contact information, website details and author profile page at http://www.pride-publishing.com